Birdsong

on

Holbeck Moor

Billy Morris

ISBN: 9798354611881

Print Edition

The author can be contacted at
BM.Author@outlook.com and via Twitter
@Yorkshire_Tales

Billy Morris was born in Leeds, Yorkshire in 1966. He left Leeds in the late 1990's and has lived and worked in Europe and USA. He now lives in South East Asia. He wrote his first book 'Bournemouth 90' in 2021 and published the sequel, LS92, in 2022.

Part 1 -France, 1916

Chapter 1

May 1916, Northern France

Frank Holleran sucked on his clay pipe and a red glow illuminated his unkempt, bearded features in the gloomy kitchen of the Touvent farmhouse.

"This bloody wood is soaked wet through," a hunched figure kneeling by the grate of a cooking range muttered, as the first plaintive harmonica notes of the evening stirred half a dozen khaki clad men from their semi-slumber on the stone floor.

"You know what they say about a poor workman and his tools Harry." Holleran reached across to re-position a rain-soaked khaki tunic, hanging on a chairback in anticipation of the drying heat of the fire.

"What's it to be lads?" Percy Cookson cupped his hands around the harmonica and inhaled and exhaled in four short breaths, to achieve a burst of vibrato notes.

"Hello, Hello, who's your lady friend!" was the half sung, half shouted response from a small man with a thick Scottish accent slumped in the corner.

The groans and shouts of abuse from the Scot's companions were interrupted as the heavy wooden door opened with a bang and a teenager in a British army greatcoat and French fieldhand's straw hat burst into the room.

"Vehicle approaching Frank. Just turned onto the farmtrack. Sounds like one of theirs."

The young man's shouted alert prompted a flurry of movement, as the men on the floor scrambled to their feet and hurtled towards different areas of the room to locate their weapons.

"Hamish, Walter, Huggins, Richardson, cover the downstairs windows with the Chauchat gun. Percy and Ronnie, upstairs with me. Help me with the Lewis." Holleran tapped out the still-lit tobacco from his pipe into the fireplace, and the threat of imminent violence electrified the atmosphere in the cold kitchen.

Three minutes later, the sound of wood pigeons cooing in the roof eaves was disturbed by a Daimler engine revving, as the tyres of a mud spattered Marienfelde truck span in the deep puddles and ruts of the farm track.

"Hold your fire boys." Frank Holleran's voice was just loud enough for the men downstairs to hear above the sound of the advancing motor. He pulled a lace curtain aside and raised a pair of field glasses to peer down the drive at the approaching wagon.

"A dozen men...maybe fifteen...4th Bavarian Division...7th Reserve too...what the hell...5th Division uniforms as well..." Holleran began to laugh quietly as the truck approached, with a heavyset man in goggles balancing a Madsen machine gun on the cab roof, as the van lurched forward through the pot holes.

"They're not the Bosch, lads, but they're not ours either. They're fucking pirates, bandits, AWOL just like us!"

"I don't blooming well believe it..." Percy Cookson had picked up the field glasses and now trained them on the back of the truck.

"Belvere...that dirty froggy bugger. He's with them!"

2

"The bastard. He's sold us out. He's told them about the treasure!" The angry voice of Clarence Huggins from the floor below preceded a sustained report from the Chauchat gun which raked across the farmyard and caused the advancing lorry to swerve to a halt, its occupants leaping from the truck to take up defensive positions.

"He knows where it's buried Frank, that's what they're here for!" Cookson smashed a window pane with the stock of his Lee Enfield rifle and extended the barrel through the jagged glass.

"Well bugger that. I'm not spending four weeks dodging red caps and kipping in bombed out farms to let some Jerry deserters take what we've stolen." Holleran positioned the tripod of the Lewis gun on the stone window ledge and ducked out of sight behind the lace curtain.

"Hold your fire boys...let them come. Let them come."

The crack of sporadic rifle fire from behind the German truck punctuated the rattle of the idling engine, as neither side risked making the first move.

"Belvere, you thieving dog, I'll skin you alive!" Hamish Wallace's guttural Glaswegian accent caused the men on the upper floor to snigger.

The heavily accented response of 'Go and fuck yourself, British pig' prompted another stuttering explosion of fire from the ground floor. The metallic ping of bullets hitting the truck's chassis preceded the pop and hiss of a front tyre deflating. Knowing there was now no chance of retreat forced the invaders into action, and two MG15 machine guns appeared above the truck's flat bed to provide a burst of covering fire, as three figures emerged and darted towards the farmhouse, firing their weapons at hip level as they ran.

Their appearance prompted a hail of fire from the windows of the farm, causing the advancing figures to roll for cover beneath the rusting machinery in the courtyard. A momentary silence was broken as a smoke grenade arced high above the truck and bounced across the cobbles.

"Here they come lads, steady yourselves." Frank Holleran fingered the trigger of the Lewis machine gun as thick grey smoke drifted across the farmyard, obscuring the view of the truck.

A sudden loud noise and movement to his right caused Holleran to turn just in time to see Ronnie Turner fall away from the window, a gaping wound in place of his left eye socket. Percy Cookson crouched below the window, his rifle held above his head, screaming in terror as he fired blindly through the shattered glass.

Holleran gasped to control his breathing, and peered into the smoke-filled courtyard to see a dozen men rushing forward, wild eyed with adrenaline pumping, firing their weapons as they ran. Holleran steadied the Lewis gun, pushing its tripod hard against the window sill and squeezed the trigger. The first figure to emerge from the blanket of smoke had pulled his grey helmet low over his eyes and it dissolved in an explosion of metallic fragments as Holleran's bullets found their mark. The next moving target recoiled as a direct hit on his right shoulder spun him sideways. The next advancing figure collapsed forward as a bullet ripped through a shin, before Holleran was forced to duck for cover as the remaining glass in the window shattered under a hail of machine gun fire.

"You got Belvere Frank!" A shout from the ground floor was punctuated by a chilling, animalistic scream, followed by Huggins' panicked cries.

4

"They've got Hamish, Frank! They're at the door..."

His voice was lost in an explosion which rocked the farmhouse and sent a snowstorm of plaster crashing onto the heads of Holleran and the men in the bedroom.

"Clarence! Clarence?" The lack of response to Holleran's shouted question confirmed his worst fears that a grenade had taken out the men defending the ground floor.

"Damn! Cover the stairs Percy, they're coming in." Holleran tilted the barrel of the Lewis gun towards the farmhouse door and spewed a barrage of fire downwards.

It was impossible to distinguish the sound of covering fire coming from behind the truck from the reports of his own weapon, but Holleran now detected a new sound coming from the rear of the farmhouse. A steady rumble preceded the repeated sharp crack of a Vickers machine gun which was now strafing the German truck, causing the fuel tank to erupt in clouds of billowing black smoke

"My God...It's one of ours! A Sporting Forty!" Percy Cookson grinned as he peered gingerly around the window frame at the Lanchester Armoured car which was now advancing towards the burning truck.

"We're saved Frank, thank God!"

Holleran raised the barrel of the Lewis gun and picked off a German who was fleeing down the farm track.

"We're saved alright Percy, but we've got to explain where we've been for the last month...and we've also lost our bloody treasure."

Chapter 2

27 June 2016, Bus-le-Artois, France

"Everything alright Frank?" Percy Cookson clutched a bottle of red wine and swayed towards the tilting gravestone that Frank Holleran was leaning against.

"Why wouldn't it be?" Holleran drew on his pipe and continued looking away, over the roof of the farm facing the church, to the flat arable fields and the palls of smoke from the distant frontline.

"The lads think you've got the wind up about tomorrow. Is it about losing the treasure?"

Holleran shook his head. "I've not given up on that. We just need to get away again Percy. Belvere's dead but we don't know who else he told about it. We need to get back there and move it. Bury it somewhere away from the farm where we can easily find it after the war."

Cookson slumped alongside Holleran and passed him the bottle.

"Not like you to be hiding away when there's a party on, the lads have almost drunk the Corner Café dry! Thought you'd want to enjoy the last night before the big push?" Cookson looked across the churchyard to a campfire where a group of soldiers sang a drunken accompaniment to a mistuned accordian.

'Gaily we'll march to war my lads, march with a ringing cheer.

March with rifle bayonets fixed, never a thought of fear.'

Holleran shook his head and Cookson thought he detected tears in his friend's eyes.

"Are you okay old pal?"

Holleran inhaled deeply and turned to face him.

"Something bad is going to happen Percy, I can feel it. When we go over the lid this time, we aren't coming back." Holleran bit his lip then took a swig from the bottle.

"The Brass say the French have been hammering the German line with their eighteen pounders though, they'll be mincemeat before we get to them. We'll walk through the wire, you'll see."

"I know though, Percy. Whatever the Brass say, I know."

"Know what? How?" Cookson held out his hand to receive the wine bottle.

"You'll think I'm mad." Holleran smiled and wiped his eyes with the back of his hand as the song ringing across the churchyard grew louder and more out of tune.

'Cheerily marching to battle, cheerily singing our song.

Leeds boys are we, gallant and free, in duty and daring strong.'

"Come on then, let's have it." Cookson slurred and burped.

"My Grandad. He's a wiseman. You know what that is?"

"Like the ones who went to see Jesus?" Cookson took off his helmet and scratched at his thick fringe.

"No. A different sort. Some people call his type wizards."

"Does your grandad wear a pointy hat then?" Cookson was laughing now, but Holleran remained grim faced.

"He learnt from a man called Henry Harrison who was a famous wiseman in Leeds about fifty years back. My grandad can tell the future, and I think he sent me a sign."

Cookson stopped laughing and extended the bottle towards Holleran, who shook his head.

"When we had that skirmish in the wood at Montauban the other day, did you see a dog?"

"Crikey Frank, I wasn't looking for dogs. I had all on trying to keep my head down when we were copping for the thick of it from all angles."

"I know, me too. We were pinned down, I was lying in the mud and the trees were getting ripped apart by machine gun fire. There were branches crashing down all around and I looked up to check what was going to fall on me. There, in the middle of the battle, with the whizz-bangs ripping the ground up all around us, I saw a big black dog. He was just sitting there looking at me. There were rounds flying all around me and I thought, this is it, I'm going to cop a packet here, and I pushed my face into the mud. When I looked up again, the dog was gone."

"No surprise there. Gone in a thousand pieces probably." Cookson smiled again.

"No Percy. I know that black dog, I've seen it before. It was a sign. If we go over the lid tomorrow, we aren't coming back."

"But what then? There's no way we can scarper again. You know Marsden doesn't believe our story about getting caught the wrong side of the line. He's watching us like a hawk."

"Speak of the devil." Holleran nodded towards a barrel-chested man with a bushy moustache approaching across the graveyard.

"Holleran, Cookson, why aren't you with the rest of the men?"

"Just enjoying a last night of peace sarge, before we move up to the line tomorrow."

Marsden curled his lip with distaste as he looked down on the two men.

"Have you carved your name on the church Holleran? I've just spotted a dirty great FH in the stone on the back wall."

Holleran smirked. "How do you know it was me Sarge? Half the lads here have left their mark on that wall. Something to show they were here if they don't make it through tomorrow."

Marsden's moustache twitched in annoyance. "Well, you have a reprieve on that score. They're forecasting wretched weather over the next two days. The Brass are worried we'll get bogged down, so the advance has been pushed back to Saturday. We'll go over the bags at dawn on the 1st now."

"Day off tomorrow then sarge?" Cookson smiled up at the sergeant but received only a scowl in response.

"I'm watching you two ..."

"Not much to see here though is there sarge?" Holleran leant back on the gravestone and drew on his pipe, sending a cloud of smoke drifting into Marsden's face.

"You might have fooled Captain Ellis with your story of being trapped behind the Fritz lines, but you don't fool me for a minute. I know all about you Holleran..."

"We're heroes though Sarge! Mentioned in his dispatches aren't we? Must make you very proud." Cookson laughed and swigged from the wine bottle.

"What is it you think you know about me then?" Holleran didn't look at Marsden as he addressed him, keeping his gaze focused on a distant bank of dark smoke drifting across the horizon.

"I know you were involved in the riot at the Etaples Training camp for a start."

Holleran sighed and shook his head. "Everyone knows it was the Kiwis and the Northumberlands that started the bother at the Bull Ring."

"There were plenty of Leeds and Bradford Pals involved in the scrap at Pont des Trois Arches though, and I know for a fact you were there when they tried to storm the glasshouse to free the lads who'd been arrested."

Holleran smiled as he recalled a rare victory over the red caps.

"I also know about your family business, what you did before the war." Marsden rubbed at his moustache, hoping he'd get a reaction, but Holleran remained impassive, staring ahead.

"A backstreet bookie with your fingers in lots of pies, and almost all illegal. Does that sound about right?"

Holleran shrugged. "We're in Armley if you ever fancy a bet Sarge. Just ask in the White Horse, they'll point you in the right direction."

Marsden snorted and turned, calling over his shoulder as he walked away. "Just remember, I'm watching you."

Frank Holleran watched him leave and turned to Cookson.

"We need to get out of this, and I think I know how."

"No way Frank, Marsden would love to have us tied to a post at first light, we can't risk going AWOL again. We have to go over the lid on Saturday."

"Oh don't worry Percy, I won't give him the chance. I'll be going over the lid alright, I just won't be one of the first, and I won't be getting too far." Holleran tapped the Webley pistol on his belt and Cookson looked at him expectantly.

"I was talking to an SB at the field kitchen in the village. Asked him the best way to get shipped back from the line, but not cop for a Blighty wound. Just enough for a few days at a dressing station. No problem slipping away from there to move the treasure."

"What are you going to do?" Cookson watched as Holleran removed his pistol and positioned the barrel above the left edge of his boot.

"The knack is to shove it down so you can feel it on your little toe...then bang! Plenty of blood but the SB's can't tell how bad it is until they get your boot off. And they won't be doing that in No Man's land with the flak flying will they?"

"Shooting your toe off though Frank, what if you miss?" Cookson grimaced and shook his head.

"I won't. I'll go over the bags at the back, then go down after a few feet. Near enough to the trench to crawl back when I've taken the shot. Are you with me?"

Cookson shook his head. "It doesn't feel right Frank, leaving the other lads."

"It's that or die with them Percy, believe me." The two men looked over to the campfire and listened as the Pals' song filled the damp evening air.

'Now we're far from Leeds my lads. Goodbye to England dear.

Though there's a lump in our throats my lads, Pals won't shed a tear.

Conquer we will or die my lads, All hearts beat as one.

Steadily marching side by side. Leeds lads marching on.'

Chapter 3

4 July 2016, Near Serre, France

It had taken three days for the rats to fully occupy the body of George Wilson. Now, Arthur Rowley watched in horror as a twitching nose and whiskers slowly emerged from George's gaping mouth, to claw at the young soldier's white cheek and begin to feast upon his staring, unseeing eyes. Others now teemed from his chest cavity, emerging from the folds of his greatcoat. It was clear that George Wilson was being gradually hollowed out by the vermin which plagued the shell holes in their millions. Arthur lay immobilised three feet away, his legs submerged in a foul orange slurry of blood, petrol, excrement and mud.

He'd known nothing of the shell blast which had brought him here. A deafening, high pitched whine followed by a white flash and a feeling that the air was being sucked from his lungs. Then a choking blackness and unbearable pain spreading across his chest before he lost consciousness. Now, three days on, he remained where he'd fallen, caught between the Leeds Pals line and the German trenches they'd been attempting to overcome.

It had been too quiet the night before they'd gone over the lid. They'd expected the French to pound the German line for twelve hours solid before the big push, but as the night wore on, it became clear that wasn't happening. Then, at 6am, as the sun rose in a cloudless sky, the Pals stirred from a listless sleep to hear a crescendo of sound. A colossal explosion of birdsong filled the air, and it was as if every bird in France had taken to the sky to greet the new day. The troops gazed up in wonder as an unending murmuration swooped and soared above them. Then the earth shook and the air was filled with a terrible thunder, and the Pals crouched, shaking in their trench and listened to the British shells travelling through the dawn sky high above them. The vast flocks of starlings, blackbirds and larks had disappeared, to be replaced by these giant birds of destruction.

They'd expected to go before first light, with the Leeds Pals leading the 93rd Battalion assault on the German line outside the village of Serre. The Leeds boys would be followed in by the Bradford Pals and the Durham Light Infantry. At 7.30, in bright sunlight, they were still waiting for the whistle, and when it came, half the ladders sank into the mud and others snapped in the damp, leaving the first Pals scrambling and staggering uphill towards the wire.

Arthur's legs were shaking so much he struggled to move under the weight of his pack, and he only knew he'd lost control of his bladder due to the sudden rush of liquid heat in his groin. He was surprised at how far in front of him some of the lads had got, and also how high their bodies were lifted into the air when the German machine guns found their mark. He recognised Dolan, Corbett, Macklin, Thewliss, Maun and Wilson ahead of him, and watched them fall one by one, torn apart by the shrapnel which seemed to fill the suddenly darkened sky. Thirty feet ahead, he was surprised to see men standing, exposed from waist level above the trenchline, firing above the sandbags, and it took him a few seconds to realise he was so close to the Germans that he could hear their screams above the noise of the battle, see the terror etched on their faces. Then there was only the darkness, trying to keep his head above water, a searing chill which penetrated his bones and a terrible stench of chemicals and blood and shit and fear.

Three days on, or was it four, and the heat of the previous two days had broken in an explosion of electricity, and a downpour which raised the water in the shellhole to the level of his chest. He could move his hands now, that was a good sign, but raising his arms or moving his legs was impossible and he felt sure that his back was broken. Emboldened by Arthur's lack of movement, the rats now extended their quest for nourishment to his prone body, and he felt their sharp claws on his ears, their teeth tugging at the matted hair extending beneath his helmet, exploring the dark recesses of his soaked clothing. Anticipating that death was close, they now pushed their luck, sniffing at his lips, probing his thin moustache, excited by the blood-tinged stench of his warm breath.

A tear trickled down Arthur's left cheek and attracted an eager rodent which nipped at his skin as it enjoyed the salty moisture, and he could lay still no more and screamed in pain as he slowly lifted his right arm to brush the creature from his face.

A cat came in the early afternoon, its gore-soaked face peering inquisitively above the lip of the crater.

"Yes I'm still alive, no lunch for you here yet." The cat's tail flicked as it prowled above Arthur, and it seemed oblivious to the sporadic machine gun fire passing between the two lines of troops. Its belly was distended and at first Arthur wondered if it was pregnant, before concluding that it had merely grown fat on the corpses of his fallen comrades.

He'd assumed Captain Ellis had died at first light, having heard no sound from him during the previous five hours, but now his haunted cries could again be heard during any brief lull in the artillery barrage, crying for his parents, his brother, for his comrades fifty feet

15

away to end his suffering, suspended as he was on the wire in one hundred feet of fiery hell between the stalled British advance and the German trench line.

For three days, Ellis had provided a gruesome sport for the Hun, and Arthur could hear their distant laughter as each defender of the German trench took their turn at making the officer scream with another bullet clipping his arm, blowing away a couple of fingers, or ripping through his knee cap.

"Kill me, oh fucking kill me, please. Mother, father, please help me. God forgive me."

Ellis's cries chilled Arthur's heart and he tried to call out to the NCO from the shell hole, but his breathing was shallow, and he could barely whisper, so all he could do was listen, as the bullets slowly took Ellis apart. Then as darkness fell, the howls of the carrion dogs became louder and Arthur braced himself against the agony he felt when lifting his arms, to cover his ears, to stifle the screams as the dogs tore away at Ellis's flesh.

When the light faded on the fourth evening, Ellis had been silent since daybreak and the dogs came for Wilson, splashing in the foul slurry of the shell hole, scattering the rats and feasting on the body of Arthur's friend, close enough so he could hear their snarls and smell their evil breath. He began singing to let them know he was still alive, though every breathless word he uttered was agony.

'Now we're far from Leeds my lads, goodbye to England dear.'

The dark shape of a large black dog was tearing at the fabric of Wilson's puttees, eager to access the soft flash of his calves, and Arthur felt its weight on his own legs.

'Though there's a lump in our throats my lads, Pals won't shed a tear.'

It was a clear night and as a bright, half-moon appeared through the drifting chemical clouds above, the dogs departed, but Arthur's eyes remained tightly closed. He couldn't bear to look at what remained of Wilson in the half light.

He woke before dawn and flinched at a movement by his side, anticipating another rodent trying to breach the protective layers of his tunics. The movement was different this time though. Rather than the incessant scurrying and scratching, it felt like a nervous, tentative exploration of the shell hole. Move, move, move, pause, and repeat. Arthur shifted his head slightly but was unable to see what was moving through the mire beside him. In a brief lull in the constant boom of distant shellfire he detected a faint sound, a reedy, high pitched, rapid repetition. This was birdsong, but not the excited chatter of dawn on the first. This was a cry of panic, alarm and distress. The bird seemed to be assessing whether Arthur was a threat, and his lack of movement emboldened it, causing it to hop awkwardly onto his lower legs. A male blackbird, its left wing hanging awkwardly, its head turned away, assessing Wilson's corpse but a beady orange eye still monitoring Arthur for signs of life. The bird dragged its useless wing as it hopped haphazardly onto Arthur's stomach, and he wondered whether it had suffered an encounter with the cat or been knocked from the sky by the air-rush from an exploding shell. He closed his eyes and enjoyed the feeling of another living being on his chest as he drifted into a semi-conscious state.

The sun was higher when he opened his eyes, and the blackbird was no longer moving. He slowly and painfully lifted his head, to see it resting in his lap, its broken wing extended awkwardly out to the left and its head tucked into its chest. Arthur grimaced in pain as he lifted his right hand and extended it towards the bird, which made no attempt to escape as he gripped it hard, his fingers closing across its back, trapping its wings.

He had wondered whether it was dead, but now he held it, Arthur could feel its heartbeat. He held it in front of him and its orange eyes flashed, wild with fear, and its beak opened in an extended, silent cry of terror. The bird knew it was about to die, and Arthur closed his own eyes as he tightened his grip, feeling the tiny ribcage collapse as he squeezed hard, suppressing the urge to scream as its head fell, limp over his fingers. Arthur found his hand was shaking uncontrollably as he blindly fumbled in the kit bag by his side, locating the lock knife and flicking the blade open. After four days without food, the living bird had seemed a source of the nourishment his body craved. Now, in death, it felt only like a handful of feather and bone, and he knew he would be unable to eat it.

Killing the bird for food had made sense, but now, as he tossed its still warm corpse into the mud, the killing had become senseless, yet another wasted life, and a tear trickled down Arthur's cheek. He closed his eyes, hoping that death would come today, and take him quickly, before another nightfall and a visitation from the Grim Reaper's hell hounds, the starving pariah dogs of Serre.

Part 2 –
Leeds, October 1918

Chapter 4

"I heard what happened to your poor brother in France, Edgar. Terrible, just terrible. Words alone can't convey the horrors he must have experienced." George Cribbins lit a cigarette and struggled with the rusty catch of the small window of his cramped office.

"How long was it that he was stranded in no-mans-land?"

"Five days and four nights he spent in a shell hole with the corpse of one of his pals. He survived only by drinking the muddy water he was lying in. They managed to lay down covering fire for the stretcher bearers on the last day and they found him, babbling nonsense and shaking like a leaf." Edgar Rowley reached towards his hat on the desk in front of him and flicked some dust from the brim, and blinked as smoke from Cribbins' cigarette stung his eyes.

"He's home now, that's the main thing I suppose. How's he holding up? It can't be easy, neither for him nor for you and Eliza?" The window opened with a creak and Cribbins exhaled a ring of smoke towards the rutted gravel wasteland bordering Leeds City's Elland Road ground.

"It's like living with a ghost George. He awakes screaming in the night and we hear him pacing around, talking incessantly to some invisible presence which seems to plague him. He succumbs to exhaustion in the scullery at dawn and we wake to find him slumped in a hard seat with his head resting on the table. Even in sleep he seems tormented, as his arms and legs twitch in spasms and he mutters and moans before waking with an awful cry of terror. Then he leaves the house with barely a word to 'Liza or I, and he spends most of the day sitting on a bench next to the bandstand on Holbeck Moor, staring into space. I sit beside him sometimes and he barely acknowledges my presence, though he often asks if I can hear the birds singing."

"The birds?"

"Yes, it's a strange thing. He maintains that the birdsong was the loudest he'd ever heard on the dawn of that morning, but since then he can no longer hear it at all."

"Deafness from the shelling, I suppose?"

Edgar shook his head. "There is that possibility, but he doesn't seem unable to hear other sounds. He claims the birds just no longer sing in his presence."

George Cribbins raised his eyebrows. Edgar Rowley shook his head and looked away then spoke in a low voice, little more than a whisper.

"I love my brother, but sometimes wonder if it would be better had he followed the rest of the Pals on the first of July..."

"Followed...?" Cribbins stubbed out his cigarette in a brass ash tray and reached for another from a silver case on the desk.

"They say that every street in Leeds had at least one house with curtains drawn by the third week of July in

1916. The Telegram boys were working eighteen hour days." Edgar Rowley blinked back tears and avoided eye contact with Cribbins.

"Of course. We all know someone. The Pals were two years in the making, in ten minutes destroyed. Let down by the French."

"Let down by the bloody 'brass' George! By their own Generals. They sent those boys over the lid knowing they were walking into hell that morning." Edgar's eyes flashed with anger and his fist clenched involuntarily on the desk, and an uneasy silence descended on the cramped, wood panelled room until Crippens spoke.

"What is it I can do for you, old friend? I'm not sure how I can help?"

"I hate to ask George, but I was just wondering if there are any jobs here at the City ground you could offer Arthur? They shipped him back with an 'S' stripe, so he's not even classed as wounded. Doesn't get a proper pension as he's only seen as 'sick'. Any small wage would help, but it's really just to get him out of the house, give him a sense of purpose again."

George Cribbins tapped his cigarette on the desk and lit it, his eyes narrowing as he inhaled, causing the tip to glow orange.

"I wish I could help old chap but I'm not really calling the shots here anymore."

"I heard Mr. Chapman is required less at Barnbow now. Is it right that he'll be back in charge in the next few weeks?"

Cribbins expression drifted towards rueful amusement.

"If it were up to Mr. O'Connell, Herbert would have still been picking the team while he was also managing five hundred ammo packers for the last three years."

"Your relationship with the chairman is still not the best then?" Edgar picked his words carefully, knowing that Cribbins and his boss hated each other.

"Edgar, you really haven't a clue old friend!" Cribbins smiled, his expression suggesting he had more to say, and Edgar Rowley raised his eyebrows to demonstrate his interest.

"This isn't for publication though. It's between you and me, it mustn't end up in the Post?"

Edgar Rowley leant forward across the desk, feigning irritation that the question should even be asked.

"How long have we been friends George?"

"Must be fifteen years now, since teacher training college? Feels like a lifetime ago. How did we end up here, you a reporter, me running a bloody football club?" Both men smiled ironically at the career diversion the war had forced upon them.

"So, what's the problem with Mr O'Connell?"

George Cribbins drew on his cigarette and leant back in his chair.

"They're out to get me Edgar. That's the long and short of it."

"Get you? Who is and how?"

George Cribbins leant forward and lowered his voice.

"O'Connell has brought in an accountant. Some young chap called Delaney."

"Surely that's a good thing? You were never happy running the administrative side of the club were you? Drumming up support from local businesses, getting them to take on season tickets, that was your strong point..."

"This accountant..." Cribbins held his cigarette between thumb and index finger and raised it to his lips.

"...he's going through the books, looking at the Finances for the last two years."

Edgar Rowley shook his head and shrugged.

"And what's happened here over the last two years?" Cribbins rubbed his chin in mock rumination.

"Well, City only won the damned Midland league and the play off against Stoke to become champions of England, if that's what you mean? And with a stand-in manager picking the team to boot!"

The two men smiled in acknowledgment of what represented a remarkable achievement, even if most of England's top flight football clubs had ceased operations during the war years.

"Very true Edgar, very true. But how did we do that? Just how did City win the league?" The smile had vanished from Cribbins' face as swiftly as it had appeared. Edgar Rowley shook his head, unsure where the conversation was heading.

"Billy Hibbert, Charlie Buchan, Tommy Hampson, Bob Hewison, Fanny Walden? Our main goalscorer Jack Peart? What's the link?"

Edgar nodded his head. "Our guest players made a big difference, no doubt about that."

"Internationals. The cream of this country's footballing talent. How do you think they ended up at Elland Road?" Cribbins put out his cigarette and opened and closed the silver case without removing a replacement.

"Newcastle and Sunderland had stopped playing, we were the nearest option for their players. The munitions industry in Leeds provided them with reserved occupations, allowing them to contribute to the war effort but keep playing football..." Cribbins smiled and shook his head as Edgar offered his explanation.

"Those were just the reasons we fed to you press boys. The real answer is very simple. It's the answer to most questions, in fact. The real answer, Edgar, is money. Money and greed."

Cribbins removed a cigarette from the silver case and lit it.

"Send your brother down here on Monday, Edgar. Arthur can help old Ned sweep the steps after the Rotherham County game on Saturday. Hopefully I still have enough clout to employ new groundstaff. Anyway, I'll soon find out. I have a meeting with O'Connell in half an hour."

Chapter 5

The clang of a bell and the familiar sound of a low hum and rattle coming from Elland Road told Edgar Rowley that he'd missed the Number 5 tram to Leeds even before he'd seen the burgundy and lime-green vehicle passing the gates to the Leeds City enclosure.

"Damn it." He lit a cigarette and straightened his hat, then buttoned up his jacket. The first Northerly winds of a Yorkshire winter were beginning to chill the early October air, and he regretted not wearing his overcoat. Still, the walk into the city would do him good and as he passed the Old Peacock pub, he watched the distant tram heading past the Islington cricket ground and Beggars Hill Farm, heading towards the brickworks below Beeston Hill. He glanced at his watch. Fifteen minutes until he was due to meet Clifford at the Evening Post offices in Albion Street. Not a chance of that now. He envisaged the old reporter drawing on his pipe, tapping at his pocket watch in mock admonishment of his young colleague's tardiness. Quickening his pace, Edgar was approaching the junction with Cemetery Road when he heard a clanging bell behind him, and quickened his step to reach the stop just before the approaching tram.

He handed over a farthing to the conductor and she nodded a thank you as he climbed the wooden stairs to the top deck. In a few weeks, the winter covers would go over the front windows but for now, they were still open, and a smattering of passengers had opted for the colder, fresher air over the enclosed lower deck, with the influenza pandemic still ravaging the city. Heading for the back of the carriage, Edgar passed two ladies, their faces covered by masks, betraying their fear of the killer 'gripe' which was sweeping Europe.

As the tram rattled past the Union workhouse on Meadow road, Edgar glanced to the left towards Holbeck Moor, to the bench by the bandstand and a hunched figure in a greatcoat and flat cap, looking towards the road with unseeing eyes. His brother, Arthur. An old man of twenty two, listening for the birdsong he could no longer hear.

Edgar raised his hand in a tentative wave, but the seated figure only stared ahead, at the turrets of the foreboding workhouse building opposite the moor, and Edgar wondered what it was he could see there.

His thoughts were interrupted as a young woman swayed towards him amidst a clamour of giggles and encouragement from her four friends seated at the front of the tram. Factory girls from the uniform works in Holbeck. The girl was in her late teens, with a pretty face and long hair pinned back under her bonnet. Edgar could imagine her attracting some admiring glances when promenading on the town circuit in her Saturday night finery, but today she wore a sheen of sweat and when she smiled her front teeth betrayed the stains of a prodigious Woodbine habit. Edgar inhaled the smell of stale sweat, tobacco and an infrequent laundry regime as she gathered up her skirts and sat on the bench seat in front of him.

"Are you in 'Brotherhood?" She smiled and her eyes widened and danced mischievously.

"I'm sorry Miss, I'm not sure..." Edgar knew exactly what she meant, and the direction in which the conversation was heading.

"The Beeston Brotherhood. Conscientious objectors. Or as my friends and I call them...damned slackers!" The girl raised her voice and tilted her head to ensure her friends could hear the exchange.

"Elsie...you're a one!" They cackled and shook their heads at their workmate's coarse language.

"I'm afraid you're mistaken Miss, I'm in a reserved occupation." Edgar had been in this situation many times before and knew that keeping a cool head was vital. Otherwise, the situation could quickly escalate with other members of the public intervening on the side of the accuser.

"Reserved eh? Don't give me that. Now that 'war is almost over you 'conchies' think it's safe to show your cowardly faces again. No one will ever forget you know..."

"I was a teacher.... I am a teacher, and now a journalist." Edgar lowered his voice as other passengers were now turning to observe the proceedings and the facemask ladies scowled at him with hateful eyes.

"A journalist? You think 'pen is mightier than 'sword, no doubt?" The young woman stood and played to the gallery and her friends shrieked with laughter. Edgar remained silent.

"So you get to stay safe in Leeds for four years, a fit young chap, while my Freddie gets his bloody hand blown off in France. You think that's fair do you?" Edgar noticed tears in the girl's eyes as her voice began to crack and she struggled to retain her aggressive stance.

"I'm sorry." Edgar spoke quietly and dipped his head and didn't object, didn't attempt to push her away as the girl leant forward and pinned the white feather to the lapel of his jacket.

"What did you do in 'war, Mr. Reporter?" The girl stood over him and Edgar expected to feel the spit on his face, as usually happened. Instead she just shook her head and weaved back down the aisle to her friends as the tram rattled past the elaborate façade of the Queen's Theatre at the corner of Jack Lane, and Edgar thought about his first date there with Eliza five years ago.

Five years. Before he was a journalist; before Eliza had to go work shifts at Barnbow; before his brother's mind was ravaged by shellshock; before the flu and rationing and slackers and 'conchies'; before the Pals were wiped out on the Somme. Before the war.

Chapter 6

It was often said in Yorkshire footballing circles, that Leeds City Chairman Joseph O'Connell could fill a large room with his even bigger personality, and that certainly now felt true to George Cribbins, as his boss loomed above him across his cluttered office desk.

"You lack ambition George, always have and always will, that's your problem." O'Connell's voice was raised and Cribbins could smell the tobacco on his breath from three feet away.

"I'm sorry Joe, if you still want me to pick the team, then I have the final say on who's in the starting eleven. If you don't like my selection, you pick the team, or get Mr.Chapman to do it." It was a conversation which had been repeated on numerous occasions over the last two years. O'Connell usually got his way, but Cribbins was no longer in a mood to compromise.

"Mr. Chapman is still tied up with his war work, he's not in a position to fully manage the team again yet. Until he's back, we need to keep muddling through. I just don't understand your reticence George, the Rotherham County match won't be easy, we need to turn out our best possible eleven." O'Connell's bushy white moustache twitched with irritation at Cribbins' intransigence.

"Our best eleven Joe? Yes I agree, but the fact is that Maclachlan and Hampson are not 'ours' are they? Just as Billy Hibbert is still contracted to Newcastle and Bob Hewison to Sunderland."

"At this point, they're still available to us as guests, as you well know. As they were last season when they helped us win the league title. You do remember that famous day at Stoke less than six months ago when our boys valiantly clung on to win the play off don't you George? The greatest day in this club's history, you do recall that?" O'Connell's face reddened as his voice got louder and he hammered his fist hard on the desk.

"Of course Joe, I remember, but I'm not comfortable..."

"Not comfortable?! How many of us have been comfortable over the last four years George? Certainly not me, struggling to keep this club solvent, let alone win the damned championship. Not Mr.Chapman, forced to put his football career on hold for the war effort. Not the boys sent to France, our players...not poor Jimmy Speirs. Do you think he was 'comfortable' being torn apart by the Bosch machine guns?"

George Cribbins lowered his head. His mouth felt dry. His reserved occupation status hung like a millstone around his neck. Spared the horrors of the front, but faced with daily taunts and whispered insults.

"We need to be careful is all I'm saying."

"There you go again. Careful...a lack of ambition. Under my direction, Leeds City became champions of England. Winners without a trophy to raise. This season or next, God willing, we'll have a full fixture list again and this time when we win it, we'll damn well receive that trophy!" O'Connell lit a cigarette and walked to the window, tugging back a net curtain to gaze across the gravel behind the main stand.

"This work Delaney is undertaking though..." Cribbins looked over his shoulder at the chairman.

"Don't worry about the accountant, the books are in good order, I'm sure. And Mr Holleran will help address any problems relating to guest players expenses. He has all that covered."

Cribbins exhaled deeply at the mention of Holleran, who seemed to wield an unhealthy influence over the chairman and had been instrumental in securing agreements with most of the guest players.

"I hope you're right Joe. I just feel nervous that our player recruitment policy for the last two years seems to be based around the whims of a bookmaker from Armley."

"Alleged bookmaker George." O'Connell raised an index finger while continuing to stare from the window. "Mr Holleran is a businessman with a network of contacts across the country. He's a City fan and has our best interests at heart. Trust me..."

In the car park, O'Connell watched a young man of athletic build enter through the main gates carrying a kitbag. The door of a motor car opened slowly, and a tall man clambered out and donned a dark fedora hat. He called out to the young man and raised his walking stick in greeting.

Chapter 7

"Charlie! Charlie Cookson!" The tall man in the dark hat had appeared from the parked motor car and limped forward, aided by a stick held in his left hand.

"How do?" Cookson extended his hand in greeting and the tall stranger smiled.

"Frank. Frank Holleran. I was in France with your brother."

Cookson nodded, he recognised the name. Frank Holleran. Bookie, war hero, supposed gangster and unofficial agent to the many guest players that City had attracted over the last two years.

"I hear you have an injury, might have to miss Saturday's match?" Holleran removed his hat and pushed his long fringe back across his forehead.

"No, I'll be right Mr Holleran, I've just come down to the enclosure do some stretching on the rowing machine."

Holleran nodded and remained silent.

"So, you know our Percy then?" Cookson felt the need to break the silence.

"Served with him in 'Pals till I got shipped out. Blighty wound at 'Somme. Lost three toes." Holleran nodded towards his left foot.

"Sorry to hear that Mr Holleran.."

"Call me Frank." Holleran smiled but his eyes betrayed no emotion.

"Sorry to hear that Frank, but when you hear what happened that day, I suppose you could say you were lucky."

"No I wouldn't say that." Holleran looked beyond Cookson to the ramshackle stand where a coterie of pigeons swooped above its corrugated iron roof under a leaden grey sky.

"Just from what our Percy said in his letters..."

"Have you heard from him recently?"

"Two letters came last week, posted a fortnight apart. Buggering delays as usual."

"I need you to do something for me Charlie, it's important." The false smile had vanished from Holleran's face, and he moved closer and placed his hand on the player's arm.

"I'll try Mr. Holleran... Frank..."

"This..." Holleran nodded towards his left foot and Cookson looked down. "This wasn't German bullets that took half my foot away Charlie. Or shrapnel, or a shell blast."

Holleran paused and waited for Cookson to look up again.

"It was a British bullet that blew my toes away. Do you want to know how I know that?"

Cookson sensed the threat in Holleran's voice and guessed that he really didn't want to know, but was about to find out anyway.

"I know it was a British bullet because it came from my gun. I fired it. There's a saying you may have heard – to shoot yourself in the foot. Well, I literally did that."

The sinister smile had returned to Holleran's face and he stared into Cookson's eyes.

"I got it wrong. I only intended to nick my little toe, fill my boot with blood and get shipped back to a dressing station. Never intended to get sent back to Blighty with a wound stripe on my arm."

Cookson gulped and felt the hairs on the back of his neck prickle. Holleran was effectively admitting to desertion, an offence which carried a death sentence, and he had no wish to be party to such a weighty secret, but correctly guessed that the admission was about to get worse.

"I've been back two years Charlie, and now I have a problem." Holleran's hand moved from Cooksons arm and now rested on his shoulder. "And I need your help."

Cookson nodded and blinked nervously as Holleran stared hard into his eyes.

"The war will soon be over. Fritz is on the run and the boys will soon be coming home. Twenty five thousand already, so I read in the Post yesterday. Most of our old gang are either back in Blighty, or in hospital, blind or handicapped, or in a million pieces scattered across a French field. Your Percy is the last man standing. The last one of our group on active service in France."

"He's been lucky. Four years without a scratch..."

Holleran interjected quickly to make clear this wasn't a discussion on Percy's good fortune and courage.

"I've been writing to him, but all I get back is a Field Service postcard with the box saying 'I am quite well' ticked. Most of my letters probably don't get through as I'm not a family member. I need you to convey an urgent message."

Cookson nodded and Holleran looked furtively over both shoulders before leaning in towards him.

"The fact is Charlie, your brother is no more a war hero than I am. He and I, along with a band of likeminded individuals, took advantage of the state of lawlessness and general anarchy in Northern France to compensate for the loss of income and liberty we'd suffered due to the war. We became outlaws, renegades, bandits, call it what you will. We operated between the shifting front line, liberating valuables from chateaus and grand farm houses, country estates and government buildings. We accumulated quite a haul. A small fortune in fact, of jewellery, gold, diamonds and cash. We had it hidden in an old farmhouse we were using. The plan was to bury it somewhere well away from the line and go back for it after the war. Unfortunately, we were inadvertently 'rescued' before we got 'chance."

Charlie Cookson shook his head. "So when Percy was lost behind the German line for a month, and they fought their way back to the battalion...the medal?"

"I'm sorry, old pal. All a load of bloody codswallop." Holleran's smile for once seemed genuine.

"So what is it you need?" Cookson was struggling to comprehend that his brother, the war hero, was a fraud and a crook. The mention in dispatches, the photo and write-up in the Post, were all a sham.

"I need you to make sure Percy understands that he has to go back for the treasure and bury it somewhere safe where we can get it after the war. He needs to know that he's our last chance. Obviously, it needs to be worded more subtly though, or he'll end up facing the squad at dawn."

35

"But what if he's nowhere near the place? What if he can't get away from his detachment? What if..."

"He'll find a way. He has to. Write the letter today. I'm relying on you."

Holleran released his grip on Cookson's shoulder and limped towards the car without looking back, calling over his shoulder.

"Be sure to write today Charlie. The clock is ticking."

Chapter 8

"Well, well, well, whatever do we have here? Looks very much like a junior sports reporter to me, maybe even the one I was meant to be meeting half an hour ago." Clifford Ellington leant back in his chair and drummed his fingers on his sizeable girth.

"Twenty minutes Cliff…and I'm sorry, I missed the tram." Edgar Rowley removed his hat and tossed it onto a desk cluttered with newspapers and stacks of papers concealed in Manila files.

"What happened? Did you get way-layed in the fleshpots of Domestic Street?"

"Way-layed on the ruddy tram more like." Edgar removed the white feather from his pocket and crunched it in his fist before dropping it in a waste bin.

"Ouch. Another feather eh? Don't take it to heart old chap, it'll all soon be over, but I must admit, I'm glad I'm too old and decrepit to be considered for any action."

"People won't forget though Cliff. There are grudges which will be held for decades. I'll always be known as 'one of them'.

Clifford nodded and reached for a type written document from the desk in front of him.

"Have a look at this, take your mind off the feather business."

Edgar picked up the piece of paper headed 'Leeds City Police'. "Another animal slaughter?"

"They're calling him The Beast Slayer now you know."

"Who is?" Edgar laughed and shook his head and Cliff smirked with mock modesty.

"All good crime stories need a headline Edgar, and Gorman's got a bee in his bonnet over this. Wants me to schlep out to Bramhope to talk to the bloody farmer."

"Why? It's not hard to work out is it? Two years of rationing have driven a thriving black market in fresh meat. Someone will have made a packet from this bullock." Edgar tossed the report back onto the desk.

"Well, yes, that's what I've been saying for the last couple of months. Unfortunately, this follows the same pattern as the gelding at Garforth and the dozen sheep at Tong. No butchery as such, throat cut cleanly and the rib cage ripped asunder and as far as the vet could deduce, only the vital organs taken."

"So what does Gorman think?"

Clifford stood slowly and winced as he rubbed his knee.

"Damned gout's back. Bloody agony."

"All those three hour lunches at the Bull and Mouth, Cliff." Edgar smiled at his colleague's discomfort, and the old reporter limped to the window and looked out at the lunchtime shoppers hurrying along Albion Street.

"He's talking about witchcraft son, and I'm starting to wonder if he may be right."

"Witchcraft? Black cats and broom sticks?" Edgar was laughing but Clifford maintained a straight face.

"Witchcraft appears in many forms." He opened his desk drawer and removed a bottle of whisky, which he delicately trickled into a glass of water.

38

"When I was a young reporter, even younger than you are now, you would be amazed by the amount of sorcery and spell casting that went on in Leeds. After the Dove case, Leeds had become notorious for its witches and wizards."

"I've read about that. Dove poisoned his wife didn't he? There was nothing magical about it." Edgar shook his head as Clifford picked up his glass and walked to the window.

"Henry Harrison. Have you heard of him?"

Edgar shook his head.

"The wizard of the South Market. Dove had fallen under his influence when he killed his wife. He claimed that it was Harrison's spells which killed poor Harriet."

"Not the best defence really, was it? Dove ended up on the gallows at York didn't he?"

"Impressive young Edgar, you know your Leeds crime history, but I fear, not the full story. Harrison was never brought to trial, and he continued to ply his trade around Leeds, spawning a cottage industry of copycats, charlatans and rogues, following in his footsteps."

"But that was nearly sixty years ago. No one believes that nonsense now."

Clifford turned back from the window and rinsed his gums with his drink.

"In hard times, people believe what they want to believe, they revert to the old ways, the beliefs that their parents and grandparents held. And Lord knows, the last few years have been too bloody hard for everyone. When folk feel that God has forsaken them..."

Clifford paused and Edgar raised his eyebrows to encourage him to continue.

"When people feel that God is looking away, there's a danger that they'll seek help from the other side."

"You mean...?"

Clifford turned back and gazed out of the window.

"You know what I mean Edgar. Who I mean. Now, will you help me on this story? There's no way I can ride a tram then an omnibus to Bramhope with this ruddy knee."

Chapter 9

The ship pitched and rolled and creaked and groaned and closer at hand, in the darkness, the sound of retching, and crying, hushed conversations and shouted insults.

Eight hundred Leeds lads crammed below decks on HMS Shropshire, two days at sea, probably Bay of Biscay now, so the sarge said. Maybe four more days to Port Said, maybe five. Or six. To the Suez canal and the Turks. Action at last after Colsterdale and Wiltshire.

The creaks and the groans, the screams and the laughter. Jokes and nightmares.

Ighty-iddley-ighty, Carry me back to Blighty, Blighty is the place for me. Put me on the train for London town. Fucking shut it Dobson. Laughter and tears. Drop me anywhere, I don't care! If it's Piccadilly, The Strand or Leicester Square.

The smell of oil and paraffin and shit and sweat. Rolling more now, perspiration soaked hands clinging to the bunk. You make sure you don't piss yourself up there Arthur.

Creaks and groans, pitching and rolling. We're going in circles. Zig-zagging without lights to avoid the U-Boats. Pea-souper out there tonight.

All I want to see is my best girl, cuddling up again we soon should be.... Somebody thump him one!

Laughter and tears. Heart pounding, soaked in sweat.

So it's ighty-iddley-ighty, Take me back to Blighty. Blighty is the place for me!

A deafening grinding from somewhere far below, louder, louder till it drowns out the screams. No more laughter. Tilting and tipping, sweat soaked hands let go of the bunk. Face down on the floor, nose smashed and bloody, the taste of salt water, red salt water.

To the boats boys, leave your kit bags, to the boats double quick. Warm liquid trickling into his mouth and down his legs, scrambling over bodies on the deck, up the steps. Hurry, hurry boys. Ighty-iddley-ighty, Carry me back to Blighty.

Man the boats. Stand in line. Through the fog, light and sound. Screams and screams. No laughter now. Two ships starboard. Not two ships, one ship in two halves. Sliced in two. Screams and shouts. Sauvez Moi. A baby crying. Zig zag in the darkness, lights too bright now. Into the boats, into the sea, icy cold, teeth won't sit still.

Lights too bright, into the sea. Sauvez moi. Sauvez les enfants. Ighty-iddley-ighty, Carry me back to Blighty. Shropshire afloat. Darjurjura sinking. Save the children. Bodies floating, left and right. Save the children. But all I want to see is my best girl, cuddling up again we soon should be. Pull her aboard, eyes wide open, never to see again. And the child, limp in his arms, eyes staring, unseeing. Men crying, heads in hands. Arthur watching, waiting for the wave. Washing them all away, washing them clean again. Ighty-iddley- ighty. Carry me back to Blighty.

"Arthur...Arthur! Wake up! You're having a nightmare." Arthur Rowley's mouth was so dry he couldn't speak as he looked towards his brother, silhouetted in the doorway.

"I'm sorry Edgar." He whispered, and turned away to face the window.

"Don't worry old pal, you just gave Eliza a turn, screaming out. Do you want me to sit a while?"

Edgar Rowley looked down at his brother, blankets over his head, breathing hard, body rising and falling in the orange glow from the gaslight outside the window, knowing that he would receive no response and that for Arthur, sleep would remain elusive for the rest of the night. His memories would see to that.

Chapter 10

"Terrible crowd on the enclosure on Saturday, what did they call, a couple of thousand?" Edgar Rowley licked the nib of his pen to stimulate the ink flow and opened his notebook.

"I don't know what we have to do to get the spectators down here Edgar, it's a thankless task." George Cribbins lit a cigarette and sat back in the chair opposite his friend." A good result though, not withstanding the injury to Hewison of course."

"What's the news on that? Is it a fracture?" Edgar poised with his pen above the notebook page.

"Unfortunately yes. Awful luck. On his first game back too. Poor old Bob, the other chaps were so upset for him."

"And your tactical switches worked well..."

"Thank God we have Hampson who can play virtually anywhere on the field. I moved him from right half to outside left. If I can use our own lads instead of guest players, I will do, no matter what Mr. O'Connell says."

"And what have you got for me regarding the return game on Saturday?" Edgar didn't look up from his notepad as Cribbins sighed.

"As usual, we're struggling to make up the numbers if I'm brutally honest, Edgar. Obviously Hewison is out. Billy Hibbert has turned his ankle, Millership has a sore knee, Tommy Lamph is struggling to secure time off from his munitions work. Billy McLeod is available though and I think Stan Robinson will play at Outside-Left."

Edgar Rowley scribbled down the details as Cribbins stood and walked over to the window to see the stumbling figure of Arthur Rowley pushing a wheelbarrow across the pock marked gravel alongside the Elland Road main stand.

"It's terrible Edgar, I can't imagine how hard it must be for you, and the biggest tragedy is that there are hundreds like him in Leeds, and thousands, tens of thousands across the country." George Cribbins pulled hard on his cigarette as he peered round the net curtains.

Edgar stood and moved towards the window to observe his brother trying to maintain control of the barrow of refuse, swept from the terraces of the enclosure. Arthur's lips moved quickly and he appeared animated in his conversation, which was accompanied by violent head shakes and facial contortions. It would simply appear that he was involved in a lively altercation, if there were another person present.

"That's how he is." Edgar spoke quietly. "He appears tortured in his every waking moment, and even in the brief periods that he sleeps he rarely rests for long before his terrors emerge. The only time I see him still is when he sits on the moor, and then he seems in some kind of trance."

"Ned will take care of him here. He lost a boy in the South African war, so he understands the horror of conflict. I'm just sorry we can't give Arthur anything full time, but obviously times are hard now. Maybe once the war is over..." Cribbins smiled and Edgar nodded.

"I appreciate it old mate. Anything to give him a reason to get up each day is a help."

As he spoke, Edgar noticed a subtle shift in his friend's demeanour. Cribbins moved closer to the grimy window pane, his eyes narrowed and his lips tightened.

"Who's that?" Edgar peered over his shoulder to observe a tall man in a dark fedora hat clambering from a motor car. Arthur stopped pushing the wheelbarrow and turned to face the man, who limped towards him with a walking cane in his left hand.

Chapter 11

"Arthur? Arthur Rowley? It is you isn't it...?" The tall man with the hat and the walking stick was smiling as he approached, and his face triggered a brief flicker of recognition before it was lost in the confused fog of Arthur's memory.

"It's Frank, Frank Holleran, from the Pals. You remember me don't you? Bugger me mate, It's good to see you again, how are you?"

The question didn't require an answer as Arthur recoiled when Holleran reached out to shake his hand.

"Frank? I think I remember..."

"Course you do, you were there the night we stole the farmer's tractor from outside the pub at Middleham when we were training at Colsterdale..." Frank laughed and Arthur looked down at his own shuffling feet.

"And we were on the same lifeboat after we hit that French mail ship on the way to Egypt, remember, you and me were pulling those poor Froggies out of the water..." Frank's voice trailed off as he saw a slow tear trickle down Arthur's cheek.

"You've had a bad time of it mate, we all have, but at least we survived eh?" Frank placed a hand on Arthur's shoulder and felt him tremble.

"Look at me. A bloody cripple! Lost half my foot when we went over the top on the first, but I suppose I got lucky compared to a lot of the lads. What was your story that day? I was at a dressing station behind the line by midday, and back in Blighty three days later so I never found out what happened."

Arthur looked up briefly, then stared at his feet again, as his chest began to heave and he gasped for breath between loud sobs.

"Arthur...I'm sorry, old pal, I really am, I wouldn't have asked..." Frank knew now that it was too late, as Arthur's tears flowed loudly and he sank to his knees and rested his head on the gravel.

"Please get up Arthur, it's okay. We're alive. Most of our friends aren't, we have to be thankful for that." Frank sank to his knees and stroked Arthur's back and removed his cap to ruffle his greasy hair.

"I'm not though." Frank only caught the tail end of the whispered words.

"What's that mate?"

Arthur pulled himself upright and the two men faced each other, standing in the puddles in the shadow of the main stand of the Elland Road enclosure.

"I'm not thankful Frank. I know I should be, but I don't want to live anymore... I just want it to be over."

"Don't talk like that Arthur. We survived for a reason. All of us that came home did, you just need to find the reason. Believe me, it's fate that we survived." Frank Holleran reached out and gripped Arthur's hands, looking hard into his eyes.

"No. It's a mistake, I wasn't meant to come back. They should never have brought me back here." Arthur's chin fell onto his chest and again his body was wracked by loud sobs.

"Everything is for a reason mate." Holleran paused and took a deep breath and spoke slowly.

"Listen to me Arthur. I can help you. Sometimes we need a different kind of help to that the medics can give you. From a higher power if you like..."

"I'm done with churches Frank." Arthur didn't look up as he shook his head.

"I'm not talking about church. Quite the opposite in fact. I want to introduce you to someone special, my grandad. He was a landlord in Armley, and a bookie. He's also a wizard."

Chapter 12

"This is Arthur mam, an old mate from the Pals. As I told you, he's had a rough time of it. Needs a bit of help to get back on his feet."

Kitty Holleran put down the pint pot she'd been drying on her apron and turned towards the front door of the White Horse. A cart pulled by a skeletal pony rattled down Armley Town Street, and her eldest son stooped to enter the dark tap room, his arm wrapped protectively around the shoulders of a sallow faced young man.

"Nice to meet you Arthur. Have you ever worked a bar?" Her loud, confident voice seemed to unsettle the newcomer and he twitched and shook his head, his eyes remaining fixed upon his own feet.

"No matter. We can always use a fit lad around the place. You can wash up and help the dray man with the barrels."

"Thanks Mam. There's also the other thing I mentioned..." Frank Holleran raised his eyebrows and nodded toward a door leading off to the side of the bar.

"All in good time Frank. We need to...get to know Arthur first, and he us." Kitty motioned towards the door with her eyes.

"Arthur, Polly here will let you know what needs doing."

A moon-faced girl with a wide chin and ginger hair emerged from behind the bar and smiled at Arthur who glanced towards Frank, as if seeking his approval.

"Go on Arthur, Poll will sort you out. And don't worry, I'll fix it for you to see Grandad." Frank winked and followed his mother through a door next to the bar and up a wooden staircase.

Emerging into a brightly lit room, Frank's eyes stung in reaction to the pall of cigarette smoke that hung beneath the flickering gas lights. Two men sat behind a long oak desk, upon which sat three telephones. Both the men, jackets removed and shirt sleeves hoisted to elbow level, each held a telephone receiver to their ear and whispered instructions to a middle-aged woman who scribbled urgently in a thick ledger. In the corner of the room, a ticker tape machine whirred and spat its output into the waiting hand of an elderly man with a pair of glasses balanced on his nose end. Seated before him was a teenage girl who hurriedly scratched away at a large notepad.

Away to the right in the doorway of an adjoining room, Kitty Holleran stood, arms folded and scowling. In front of her, an enormous, middle-aged man with a shaved head and florid face stood over a cowering figure in his mid-twenties who was secured to a wooden chair by three thick leather straps. His left eye was swollen closed and a thin rivulet of blood dripped from his nose.

"What do we know then?" Frank Holleran addressed his mother.

"Mr.Sledge has been his usual persuasive self, but young Osborne here is still denying tampering with the bag."

Frank Holleran stepped forward and the man in the chair flinched.

"Please Frank, I don't know what went wrong with the clock, I really don't. You have to believe me." He began to cry, and the bald man placed a hand on his head and gently ruffled his hair.

"How long have you been the runner at the bootlace factory?" Frank lit a cigarette and flicked the match towards the man's feet.

"Eight months now Frank, and there's never been a problem with the bag, you know that..."

"Eight months of 10% on, what, six or seven quid a month, that's probably as much as your wage at the works." Holleran pulled up a wooden chair and sat facing the shaking man.

"I do alright yes, but I always check the bag is locked properly, always make sure the clock is right when the bag gets locked, I know how important it is..."

Kitty Holleran caught the eye of the bald giant and nodded towards the man in the chair. Frank Holleran looked on as a vicious uppercut broke the man's jaw and deposited him in a crumpled heap on the floorboards.

"You're lucky today." Frank Holleran stood above the sobbing figure lying before him. "I don't believe you're clever enough to fix the clock bag. Next time though...just make sure there isn't a next time. Mr Sledge will take you down to the infirmary."

"You're going soft son." Kitty Holleran smiled and shook her head as she followed Frank out of the room.

"He didn't rig the bag ma, he's too daft..."

"I don't mean that, I'm talking about bringing lame ducks home."

Frank turned and faced his mother.

"You weren't there, you don't understand."

Kitty Holleran shrugged. "What's done is done. We can't help every boy who has come back ruined by the war Frank. We have enough problems of our own."

"Have they been in touch again?"

"What do you think? We're overdue on the payments. Mr Sledge was told there was a Chinaman in the New Inn asking questions about placing a bet the other day."

"So?" Frank stubbed out his cigarette and flicked the tab end onto the floorboards.

"It's their way of letting us know they're here, in Armley, watching us. The debt is getting bigger everyday Frank, we're making no inroads into it."

"It will be right mam. I told you, I've got a fortune stashed away in France. Enough to settle our debts twice over and buy 'whole of bloody Manchester off the chinks."

"In France..."

"It won't be long mam, I promise. I'm getting word to Percy. He's a good lad, he'll move 'treasure, the war will be over by Christmas and come Spring we'll be back over there with a gang of lads and a load of shovels!"

Kitty Holleran sniffed. "We can't rely on buried treasure Frank. We need to keep making the payments until we can deliver a big enough score to clear the debt. I hear Mr. Chapman is on his way back to City. Is that going to be a problem?"

Frank Holleran lit another cigarette.

"That's not the problem mam. I've called the shots at Elland Road for two years. That isn't going to change now. The problem will come when the war ends and the guest players go back home. We're going to need a new plan then."

Chapter 13

Arthur Rowley pulled the muffler tight around his neck and fumbled in the pocket of his overcoat for a pair of gloves which weren't there. The beginning of November had brought the first frost of winter and the smoke from the hearths of Holbeck and Beeston tinted the air around the Elland Road ground a pale yellow.

He blew on his hands then gripped the handles of a wooden wheelbarrow filled with cigarette packets and beer bottles, swept from the steps of the enclosure. The barrow squeaked and the wheel wobbled and Arthur focused his attention on the rutted gravel which surrounded the ground, taking care to weave between the pot-hole puddles.

"Arthur...Arthur Rowley isn't it?" He turned to see a face he half recognised emerging from the changing rooms beneath the main stand. Arthur paused, and as usual, his mind was unable to straighten the zig zag lines of time and place which form memories and recollections. For him, that clarity of thought was no longer possible.

The man extended his hand and spoke softly. "Charlie. Charlie Cookson. I play for City."

Arthur lowered the wheelbarrow and slowly attempted to raise his right hand, but the tremors were uncontrollable and both men stared as Arthur's arm jerked back and forth and his hand shook violently.

"I'm sorry." He whispered and stared at his own feet.

"Don't worry pal, I heard you copped a packet at the Somme." Cookson withdrew his hand quickly and grimaced at his error. Everyone knew you didn't try to shake hands with a shellshock victim.

"I heard you were helping out here and I wanted to tell you..." Cookson's voice cracked and he looked away as Arthur looked up from beneath the peak of his cap.

"My brother Percy, you served with him in the Pals."

"Percy..." Arthur half remembered. Rolling hay bales down a hill at Colsterdale. A drunken bike ride at Etaples. Giving a French toddler the kiss of life in a lifeboat on a cold, foggy night in the Bay of Biscay."

"Percy Cookson. From Disraeli Terrace in Hunslet. He mentioned you in some of his letters. You were friends."

"Yes. Percy..." Arthur nodded and a half smile appeared on his face and his eyes blinked so fast they were more closed than open.

Charlie Cookson smiled too and attempted to speak but his words were lost in a loud sob.

"He's dead isn't he?" Arthur's face remained expressionless. Four years ago, he'd only endured the death of his parents. Now almost everyone he knew was dead.

"No...no, he's alive, he was listed as missing, but I just got word. He was wounded at Bailleul the other month. He's lost both his legs. It's terrible, he's only twenty one. But at least he's coming home Arthur. At least he survived."

"I'm happy for you that he's safe now... I'm sorry for Percy." Arthur stooped to pick up the wheelbarrow, and Cookson placed a hand on his arm.

"Our uncle has a pub. The Timble Inn out past Otley. It's lovely out there. On the moors, peaceful. We used to spend the holidays there when we were boys. I'm going to take Percy out there when we get him home. Why don't you come too? You'd be company for each other. I'm sure it would do you a world of good."

Arthur looked away and nodded then nudged the wheelbarrow forward. Charlie Cookson watched him picking his way through the pot-holes, the wheel squeaking on the front of the barrow.

"I'll let you know when he's home. Think about the pub Arthur."

Charlie called after the hunched figure pushing the barrow, but Arthur kept his head down, dodging puddles, wheel squeaking, and Charlie knew that his brother's war may be over, but Arthur's would never end.

Chapter 14

The door opened with a creak, even before Arthur had reached the top step of the staircase which led to an attic behind the White Horse pub on Armley Town Street.

He took a step back as a long, thin face with receding white hair peered around the door frame to observe him. An old man, tall but stooped, wearing a collarless white shirt and with braces hanging limply from a pair of baggy pin striped trousers.

"I knew you'd arrived. They told me." The old man's voice was deep and adopted a tone somewhere between disinterest and vague hostility. He turned and led the way into the darkened room.

"Tea?" A rusting kettle whistled on a single flaming hob, and the old man stooped beneath the angled roof of the attic to retrieve a cup from a chipped wooden cupboard.

Arthur stammered an inaudible reply but the old man was already pouring the steaming contents of the kettle.

"Sit." He nodded towards a hard backed chair and Arthur shuffled across the room, as the old man stoked the glowing embers in a grate which provided the only light in the gloom.

"My grandson tells me you're suffering from your time in France." The old man arranged the cushion on a threadbare armchair and sat opposite Arthur, taking a noisy sip from his mug as he observed his visitor.

"I...I have shellshock." Arthur's mouth felt dry and the smoke from the fireplace stung his eyes.

"Ah, yes, shellshock. That's what they call it nowadays." The old man smiled and reached out to take hold of Arthur's hand.

"Your skin is cold. Cold and clammy. Why do you think that is?"

Arthur shook his head. The old man's hand felt warm and his grip was firm. Arthur sensed that he couldn't withdraw if he tried.

"How many men did you kill in France?" His eyes seemed to look beyond Arthur.

"I...I don't know...I never wanted..."

"Of course you didn't. No one did. But the fact remains that you've killed men. You've taken the lives of boys just like you. Young men with mothers and brothers, wives, children, hopes and dreams. They could have been your friends. They could have been you."

A tear trickled down Arthur's cheek and his lip trembled.

"I don't know if I did. I never got that close..."

"Oh but you did." The old man sat back and again looked beyond Arthur.

"You killed seven men in France. I know that."

Arthur shook his head and began to sob.

"I don't know..."

"I know. I know because I can see them." The old man lifted his hand and extended his palm towards the dark room.

"They told me you were coming." The old man's tone was one of sadness and Arthur felt the hairs on his neck prickle.

59

"How old are you?

"Twenty two." Arthur whispered, peering into the gloom, hoping not to see what the old man could.

"Probably older than all of them. This boy, a tall blond lad with a simple face and big ears, doesn't look any older than fifteen or sixteen."

Arthur covered his face with his hands and the sound of his sobs filled the room.

"You shot him twice in the gut. It was in a copse of trees at the top of a hill in the rain."

"At Courcelles. I remember." Arthur's voice was no more than a whisper.

"He bled to death eventually, but it took the best part of a day. He's smiling now. Says that a lovely rainbow appeared through the clouds at the end. That's the thing, you see. They bear you no malice. It was fate that their lives would end and yours would continue...in a fashion."

Arthur rocked in his chair, the sound of his tears filling the room.

"But although they wish you no ill, the fact is that they remain with you. Their souls are inextricably linked to yours. Unfortunately, that means that their pain and suffering, the terror they felt, their loss, their grief, it all becomes yours to carry. The army don't want you to know that, so they call it shellshock.

"So I'm haunted. That's what's wrong with me? Is that why I can't hear the birds singing anymore?" Arthur peered through the gloom at the old man, who now slung the dregs of his cup into the fire.

"It's a bit more complicated than being haunted, but essentially yes. Your past actions are casting a dark shadow around you, which will mean you are precluded from the pleasures of life. Laughter, happiness, the enjoyment of simple things such as hearing the birds sing."

Arthur nodded. It made sense. Nothing had felt the same since France.

"Frank said you're a wizard. Is that true?"

The old man slowly lifted himself from his chair and picked up a poker to prod the fire.

"Wizard, witch, water-caster, astrologer, charmist, spell-caller...these are all words and phrases used to describe a man like me. However..." He turned to face Arthur and raised the poker. "All these things, these names, can be better described as wisdom. I am what used to be known in the old days as a Wise Man.

He stooped to replace the poker then turned to face Arthur.

"I was born with a full set of teeth. My grandmother delivered me and told my mother that I'd been here many times before, as soon as she looked into my eyes. Before I was five years old, I told my mother that our neighbour would soon die in a fire. A week later he perished when a boiler exploded at his factory. As a boy, I had visions. I saw things before they happened. I terrified my own mother, so she took me to a man they called the Wizard of the South Market, Henry Harrison, to cure what she saw as an affliction, a possession, but he recognised as a gift. He took me on as his apprentice. I learnt everything I know from him."

"So he taught you magic?"

"Men can't perform magic, not even the conjurers at the Empire and the Hippodrome. Men need knowledge of the old ways, the time before medicine and scientists and doctors who talk of 'shellshock'. The remedies and cures that our ancestors relied on for thousands of years, remedies they now call 'spells' and 'charms'."

The old man smiled to himself and sat back in the armchair.

"And when we don't know the answer, we contact those who do." He raised his arm and again extended his palm and looked around the room.

"The ghosts?" Arthur could feel his heart beating hard in his chest, but still, he felt calmer.

"Not ghosts. Guides. Every Wise Man needs a guide on the other side. My guide is Clem." The old man stood and moved slowly across the room to a mahogany dresser on the far wall.

"Will I see Clem?" Arthur realised that his speech seemed to be less impeded by the stammer which had appeared the day he'd been pulled from the trench.

"I hope for your sake you won't. Clem only shows himself at times of great danger, usually when death is close." Arthur watched as the old man rummaged in a drawer and removed a small hessian bag.

"Wait here." The old man shuffled from the room and Arthur listened to his heavy steps on the stairs and shrank into his chair, his eyes scanning the dark recesses of the room, hoping not to spot the lurking spirits of the men he'd killed.

Ten minutes later and Arthur's new calmness had vanished. His tunic was soaked in an icy sweat and his hands shook uncontrollably once more. The absence of the old man seemed to make the attic darker and drop the temperature by several degrees. A pervading sense of death had filled the room and Arthur could feel the ghosts getting closer, trying to be part of him, to feed off him, to experience life again through him. He felt drained when the door opened with a bang and the old man entered carrying a small parcel.

"Take this. Put it under your bed, directly below your pillow."

Arthur reached out and took the parcel, wrapped in the hessian bag, in both hands.

"What is it?" The old man was shaking his head in the gloom before the question was uttered.

"That's not to know. This will help you. It will prevent you suffering harm from the negative energies the spirits bring. They don't want to hurt you, but sometimes..." The old man's voice trailed off and he reached into the back pocket of his trousers and withdrew an envelope.

"Place this under your pillow, above the parcel. It's the second part of the charm. Again, don't open it."

Arthur took the envelope and put it in his jacket pocket, then stood to leave. The old man shook his hand and nodded towards the door.

The familiar creak heralded the door closing behind Arthur as he made his way down the stairs. He heard the creak again as he reached the bottom step.

"Arthur..."

He turned to see the long, grey face of the old man peering round the door frame.

"Spray the sack with bleach every three days. After a month, take it after dark and bury it in a field without trees or hills. Then come and see me again. Good luck."

Chapter 15

The heat of the sun prickled Arthur's bare chest and he flicked at a fly attracted to the sweat on his brow. He opened his eyes momentarily, but the glare was too harsh and he quickly closed them again. He licked at his cracked lips and enjoyed the sensation of the dry, breeze-blown grass brushing against his bare skin.

"Here, drink." The words were whispered lightly, and he felt the metal cup on his lips and opened his mouth to receive the ice-cold liquid. Again, he tried to open his eyes and the figure leaning over him was visible only in silhouette against the sun. The figure giggled playfully.

"Irene? Sweetheart? Is that you? You're still my best girl you know."

But the laughter wasn't hers and the figure withdrew the cup and crouched at his feet. Arthur sat up, resting on his elbows. A cold rivulet of sweat threaded its way down his spine and he shivered.

The boy was in his late teens. Blond hair shaved at the sides but left in an unruly mop with a thick fringe which stuck to the perspiration on his forehead. He grinned, white teeth prominent below thin lips and sunken cheeks pitted with acne scars.

"Who are you?"

The boy pushed his hair back from his eyes and laughed and took a swig of water from the metal cup. He, too, was bare chested, and like Arthur was wearing Khaki puttees and boots caked in dry clay.

Arthur looked around. They were in a shell hole, but the water and mud and blood were gone, replaced by scrubby grass and dandelions. He could hear the buzz of insects, but it was the sound of lazy bumble bees, not swarms of flesh-hungry bluebottles. The boom and crack of guns had been replaced by the sound of birdsong once more and Arthur closed his eyes and savoured the mellow, flute-like verse of a distant blackbird.

"Can you hear the birds?" Arthur smiled and faced the blond-haired boy.

"I can't hear anything. You've made it too hard for me." The boy looked sad now and Arthur wanted to ask what was the matter, but a large black dog had joined them in the trench. It sat next to the boy, observing Arthur as the boy gently stroked its head."

"Is that your dog?"

"No. I think he's come to tell me it's time." The boy began to cry, and the dog stood, its tail wagging gently.

"Don't cry, the war is over." Arthur extended his hand and the boy tried to reach out, but the dog gripped his arm in its jaws and the boy screamed in pain. Arthur tried to stand but found he was unable to move. Raising his arms or moving his legs was impossible and he felt sure that his back was broken.

More dogs came now, and the blond boy sat, wide eyed and mouth agape in horrified surprise as they took him apart, bit by bit. The first dog tore away his right arm and another animal, a stringy tan mongrel tussled with it over the prize, both dogs snarling and slavering in a macabre tug-of-war.

"No!! Leave him...Get away!! Arthur screamed and the boy now lifted his head and smiled at him.

"Do you remember me now?"

"No! I don't know you...who are you?" Arthur sobbed and although he couldn't feel his legs, he could feel the heat of the urine soaking his underwear.

"You killed me once Arthur. And now you're leaving me in the dark, you're killing me again."

"Arthur! Arthur! Wake up...you're dreaming again. It's okay. You're safe. Everything is alright."

Arthur opened his eyes and caught his breath. In the glow of the flickering landing light, he could see his brother, and behind him, the worried face of Eliza.

"I'm sorry Edgar...Eliza. I've wet the bed again. I'm so sorry." Arthur turned over and reached under the pillow to take hold of the old man's envelope.

Chapter 16

11 November 1918, Armistice Day

"Oh Edgar, I wish you could have been there! Leeds has surely never seen a day like it!"

Eliza had burst through the front door of their Holbeck terraced house like a whirlwind, face flushed and bonnet askew on her head, clutching a penny whistle in her hand.

"They sounded the bell at eleven and Mr. Kearns told us the whole of Barnbow was closing down for the day. First time in four years! You should have seen the queues for the trams. Some of the girls even set off walking. Of course, with the schools still closed for the flu, all the children wanted to be involved too and by the time we reached Quarry Hill, the tram lines were blocked with thousands of people heading for the Town Hall. There must have been fifty thousand folk there Edgar, waving flags and bunting, singing God Save the King, laughing and dancing. Then we all marched to the infirmary and they brought some of the wounded boys out into the gardens and Great George Street was so full of cheering people you couldn't even move. The sun came out too, in November! I never thought I'd see such a day!"

"It's hard to be believe, that it's all finally over." Arthur sipped at his tea as his wife flitted excitedly around the scullery.

"And you missed it! Oh Edgar, couldn't work wait for one day?"

"Cliff's bedridden with his gout. There's been another attack by this so-called Beast Slayer, and the editor wanted it writing up for today's final Post. Right out at

Otley this time. I waited an hour for an omnibus. They were all stuck with the crowds on Upper Head Row. Then of course, I couldn't get one back. Had to hitch a lift on coal truck which barely made it up the hill to the Dyneley Arms. They're building bonfires on the Chevin and up at Cookridge. The whole city will be lit up tonight!"

"There'll be fireworks on the moor too. We can go after tea can't we?"

Edgar smiled. It was good to see his wife laughing again. The truth was, that despite meat rationing and the worsening flu epidemic, which had now caused schools and theatres to be closed, the whole city seemed to be smiling again for the first time in four years.

Edgar was about to answer his wife when the creak of floorboards above caused them both to involuntarily look up.

"He was up all night again. I heard the kettle whistling at 3am and again at 5. He was back in bed when I got up for my shift."

"The night terrors. It's like the darkness torments him. He can't go on like this, but he refuses to see the doctor."

A slow procession of thudded steps heralded Arthur's descent into the kitchen, and he appeared in the doorway, unshaven face crumpled and his hair an unruly, pommade-coated tangle. He blinked quickly through livid red eyes and licked at white crusted lips.

"Eliza, Edgar...Sorry if I disturbed you in the night."

"I never heard a thing, I was dead to the world." Edgar flashed a half smile at his brother.

"Have you heard? The Germans surrendered at 5am this morning. It's over Arthur. The war has ended."

Edgar cringed and even before she saw Arthur's face, Eliza knew the words should never have been spoken. Not when Arthur's war showed no sign of ending. Edgar exchanged a glance with his wife and she looked away.

"They'll be letting off squibs on the moor later. Thought it best to let you know..." Arthur could only imagine the effect nearby explosions could have on his brother's mental state.

"I won't be here. I have to work tonight." Arthur turned on the tap and filled a metal washing bowl at the sink.

"At the White Horse? They'll be busy tonight..if they can get hold of any ale." Arthur's reservations at his brother's association with a hostelry which enjoyed such a dubious reputation were tempered by the fact that the job gave him a reason to get up each day.

"We can always get beer. Frank has a lot of contacts."

Edgar and Eliza exchanged uneasy glances.

"Are they looking after you there Arthur, treating you well?" Eliza placed a tea towel on the side of the sink as her brother-in-law leant forward and splashed water onto his face from the bowl.

"Looking after me?" Arthur turned to face her, and ran his fingers through his hair, pushing his fringe back from his face.

"Not pushing you too hard I mean...You need to..."

"They help me." Arthur seemed to surprise himself with his snapped response and turned back to lean over the sink. "Mr.Holleran helps me."

"Frank Holleran, the bookie isn't it?" Edgar tried not to adopt a critical tone.

"Not him. The old man, his grandad. He helps me."

"Helps you how, old pal?"

A silence fell on the room and Arthur picked up the towel and turned to face his brother as he dabbed at his face.

"He just helps me. He knows a lot of things the doctors don't. He looks after me, helps me remember...and helps me forget."

Chapter 17

"My God, had you taken leave of your very senses?" Joseph O'Connell's clenched fists hovered in front of his trembling, scarlet face as he paced the office in front of George Cribbins' desk in his wood-panelled office at Leeds City's Elland Road enclosure.

"Did you think Delaney wasn't going to find the payments? You made them from the ruddy club account for Christ's sake! What were you thinking man?"

Cribbins shrank back into his chair. The truth was that the stress of the job had clouded his memory. He'd been so far out of his depth in running the club in Mr Chapman's absence, that he now struggled to recall who'd been paid what and from which account.

"Mr Holleran was sometimes away on business. The guest players needed their money for rent and train fares. What was I to do? I paid them however I could, even from my own pocket, Joe. I've no idea how much money City owe me."

"How much City owe you?" O'Connell's eyes bulged in his florid face, and he lurched forward and grabbed hold of Cribbins by the lapels of his jacket. "Do you understand what you've done? You've made payments to players who aren't Leeds City employees using the club cheque book. That's an auditable trail of illegal payments. Thank God that Delaney spotted them before we filed the accounts."

"I'm sorry Joe, I really am, but I told you when Mr Chapman first went to Barnbow, I've never dealt with the playing side of the club. Season ticket sales, raffles, Christmas hampers, I was happy with that, but all this...I'm a bloody school teacher for Christ's sake." Cribbins rested his head in his hands, his elbows splayed across the desk.

"We've all had to make sacrifices George, all had to do things we didn't want to do, deal with people we would normally cross the street to avoid. To keep this club alive, I've....I only ever wanted what was best for Leeds City, and look what those sacrifices have brought us. Champions of England."

Cribbins didn't raise his head from the desk and O'Connell breathed heavily and reached into his jacket pocket for his cigarette case. He retrieved an unfiltered woodbine and tossed one across the desk.

"This is serious George, the arrangement with Mr.Holleran was that he'd use his contacts to secure the services of the guest players and he, and he alone, would be responsible for any remuneration deemed necessary. The club would never be involved in making payments to non-contracted employees, you knew that."

"That's bloody easy for you to say!" Cribbins raised his tear-streaked face. "You didn't have to deal with Jack Peart asking for his goal bonus or Tommy Mayson saying he was promised three pounds expenses for turning up for training. What could I do Joe? If I had the cash I'd pay them and Mr Holleran would reimburse me, but if I didn't..."

O'Connell exhaled loudly and blew cigarette smoke across the desk.

"This needs to go away George, and quickly. I've told Delaney to try to cover up the payments in the accounts but the cheques are traceable. If those payment stubs ever came to light..."

"They won't. The cheque book is in the safe."

"And I don't know what I'm going to tell Mr Holleran either. He was clear that his involvement mustn't be made public. The last thing he'll want is the football league auditors sniffing around."

"Why though?" Cribbins picked up the woodbine from the desk and scrabbled in the desk drawer for a lighter.

"Why what?"

"Why won't Holleran want them sniffing around? I've never understood it. Why was he involved anyway, he's not a big City fan, he rarely even comes to matches."

"He's a war hero George. Went over the lid with the Pals at the Somme, lost half his foot. He's used his contacts in the business and sporting fraternities to get those boys into reserved occupations, save them from the horrors of the war."

Cribbins raised his eyebrows, suspecting that was only half the story, and O'Connell continued.

"And Leeds City got to enjoy the talents of some of this country's finest footballers. Would we have won the league without them? I doubt it."

"And that's it?" Cribbins narrowed his eyes and pulled on the woodbine.

"As far as I'm concerned it is, yes." O'Connell tried and failed to decipher his employee's expression. "If you have anything else to say George, then spit it out?"

Cribbins shook his head.

"The arrangement we had was good for everyone. Good for the players, good for the club..."

"And good for Mr Holleran." Cribbins stubbed out the half-smoked woodbine in a brass ash tray without looking up at his boss.

"We just need to make sure that cheque book never sees the light of day George, then this will all blow over. Onwards and upwards, towards another championship for the City!"

Chapter 18

"We've lost it mam, it's gone! Jesus Christ, I'd have been a millionaire. Damn Percy Cookson and damn the bloody Bosch who took his legs. What are we to do now?" Frank Holleran sat across the bar of the White Horse facing his mother who towelled a silver tankard.

"I told you not to rely on buried treasure. It's not real, never was, we need to focus on the here and now."

"You also told me to follow my dreams and think big, and that's what I've been doing since 1914. Always looking for the opportunities , always trying to exploit this war, and I nearly pulled it off."

"We could go back to France Frank, me and you." The hulking figure of Eldon Sledge appeared at Frank's shoulder.

"It's too late Mr. Sledge, the Third Army have already retaken Bapaume. Some French family will be back to rebuild their farmhouse, resume their lives, and they'll have a nice welcome gift waiting in the cellar, if some of the Tommies didn't get their first that is."

"No more talk of treasure!" Kitty Holleran slammed the tankard down on the bar. "The Chinese have sent word that we need to deliver a big score before Christmas, or they'll call in the debt, and without selling the pub, we don't have that sort of money. Son, you need to come up with something, and quickly."

Frank Holleran lowered himself gingerly from his bar stool and grimaced as his foot made contact with the sawdust-strewn floorboards.

"The clubs are all resuming training. It's unlikely that any of the guest players will play another game for City, it's over. And another problem..."

Kitty Holleran gave a derisory snort and turned to observe a group of youths, shouting and laughing in the tap room.

"That idiot manager who's been covering for Chapman has paid some of them from the club bank account. They should be able to cover their tracks but if not, there'll be some difficult questions to answer." Frank reached for his stick and leant on the bar.

"Mother of God! Why did we get into this mess?" Kitty Holleran's raised voice caused both men to jump.

"Because it was perfect mam. My guest players made Leeds City the best team in England, they won the league! And whoever thought they were in charge, Chapman, Cribbins or O'Connell, they had no control over the players' shift work patterns or transport, and in war time, everyone knows how quickly things can change. That's why four players were missing at short notice at Barnsley in the November after I got back."

"It was a good plan, it gave us some big scores." Mr Sledge smiled.

"A 4-1 defeat that day, after a string of victories. Got some long odds on that one." Frank turned to his mother.

"It wasn't enough though. We still owe more than we can afford. We need a new plan." Kitty Holleran caught the eye of Mr.Sledge and flicked her head towards the group of youths. Sledge ambled towards them, flexing his fists in fingerless gloves, their laughter receding as he loomed over the drink-filled table.

"Just got home boys?" Frank Holleran appeared over Sledge's shoulder, looking down at the lads with their crutches and their burns, their missing arms and eyes.

"Harry got back yesterday, it's his welcome home party Mr.Holleran." A ginger eighteen year old smiled and nodded across the table to a boy in the uniform of the Yorkshire Light Infantry, a grubby grey bandage covering his forehead and right eye.

"On a spree are we?" Holleran looked at the discarded pint pots on the table.

"Nowt else to do. No work for us now 'war's over, so we might as well get sloshed on our clothing allowance payment."

Holleran turned to Eldon Sledge. "Get the boys a drink Mr.Sledge. On the house."

"But your mother..." Sledge looked nervously towards the bar.

"Leave her to me. Enjoy your drink lads." Holleran crossed the tap-room as the creak of stairs preceded a door opening to the right of the bar.

"Afternoon father." Kitty Holleran turned and addressed the old man who looked from her to Frank and spoke slowly.

"Listen to me. I have a plan. Clem came in the night. He told me what needs to be done." The old man turned and slowly headed back up the stairs.

Chapter 19

"A shoemakers awl, segments of lime, the bones of birds and rodents. You understand what these items are don't you Edgar?" Clifford Ellington ran his finger along the line of scrawled handwriting in the notebook on his desk and looked up expectantly towards his colleague.

"The contents of the farmer's dustbin?"

"You can sneer my young friend, but these seemingly random objects are props. Witchcraft accoutrements prescribed as part of a spell. I'm guessing the modus operandi was again the same?"

Edgar nodded. "Four-month-old bullock. Throat sliced open, rib cage cleaved apart and his heart removed. No butchery, no intent to remove the cuts of meat."

"Two in a week now, with the foal at Adel. It's escalating. What do the police say?"

Edgar removed his overcoat and strolled to the corner window to gaze down at the lunchtime crowds in Albion Street.

"No firm leads, as usual. However, the farmer's son noticed a stranger in the lane by the field at dusk. A large man with a bald head, described him as older than his father, wearing dark clothes was the only description given by the boy."

Clifford sniffed."Well that narrows it down to about twenty thousand men in Leeds."

"Oh, and a man was almost knocked off his bike by a truck speeding along Stairfoot Lane, which is only a couple of miles away from the farm."

"Young men in motor cars, they need to start testing folk before they can drive them in my opinion."

Edgar turned and smiled. "Not a young man though...An older man. Fat face and a bald head. Seemed to be in a great hurry."

"I'll check in with Sergeant Hobbs on that tomorrow, see if they've made any progress. Thanks for your help on this Edgar, there's no way I could have made it out to Eccup with this knee. I really do owe you one old chap."

"You can buy me lunch at the Bull and Mouth...and explain why a witch or a wizard, or whoever they are, would steal a bull's heart."

Clifford withdrew a pipe from his jacket pocket and carefully flicked open a tin of tobacco, using a small knife to spoon the contents into the pipe bowl.

"The heart of an animal is generally used as a counter-spell. The belief is that whatever threat you're facing is also driven by magic, that your foe is aided by their own witches or spirits, and they are casting spells against you. A heart pierced by metal can break such a spell and offer you protection. The heart of a young, virile animal such as a bullock is especially potent."

Edgar's smirk had dissolved into ill-concealed laughter by the time Clifford had finished his explanation.

"My word Cliff, what an education you've received at the Post!"

"I told you, things were very different forty years ago. The South Market in Hunslet was full of supposed sorcerers and spell casters. They were cheaper than going to the doctor."

"And you really think we're seeing a resurgence of that, here in this great, modern metropolis of Leeds, in the twentieth century?"

Clifford Ellington raised the pipe to his lips and teased the bowl with a lit match, inhaling and exhaling in short bursts until the tobacco glowed orange.

"Especially now. Folk have gone through four years of mental torment that no medical man could ever hope to fix. Husbands, sons, brothers, pitched into an unimaginable hell that many will never return from. Those at home feel powerless, lost, sat waiting for news, fearing the very worst. They need to feel that they're doing something, anything to try and make it right, to keep their menfolk safe..."

"So they resort to magic?" Edgar was beginning to see the logic. Had he been aware of such things when Arthur was in France, would he have turned down the opportunity to take a charm or spell to keep him safe?

Clifford puffed on his pipe and vanished into a fug of smoke on the opposite side of the desk.

"When I was in the Transvaal most of my platoon carried something in their kitbag, sent by family to keep them safe, which they most likely wouldn't want to explain to their parish priest. When you're outnumbered and under fire, you need all the help you can get."

Edgar watched a coalman struggle to coax an aged mare into movement on the street below and muttered his thoughts aloud.

"It's just a pity that the Leeds witches' charms seemed to lose all their power on the 1st of July 1916, hey Cliff?"

Chapter 20

Arthur pushed his face hard into the soft clay and held his helmet in position with his right hand as he crawled forward. The earth shook below him and although he was deafened by the incessant barrage, he was aware of every explosion from the percussive blast which shook his rib cage and rattled his teeth. Dragging his useless legs behind him, he hauled himself forward, trying to avoid the bodies until there was no way round and he was forced to crawl across them, looking away to avoid staring into his friends' unseeing eyes, his hands soaked in their blood as he clambered over them.

He reached the bloated corpse of a horse, its teeth white and prominent in its gaping mouth, and he curled in a foetal ball beside its distended stomach, shaking as he sought courage to raise his head to look towards the British line.

"Come on Arthur, not far now!" Wilson was stood on the fire step of the Pals' trench, seemingly oblivious to the shell rounds flying past him, lighting up the black night. "Twenty feet and you're home and dry!"

Arthur hauled himself over the back of the dead horse and rolled clear of the foul slurry pouring from a wound in its neck. The ground shook with a fury that seemed sure to rend the earth apart like an earthquake, and Arthur's fingers struggled to maintain a hold in the wet earth as he pulled himself forward.

"Twenty feet to go, he could smell the fire burning in the trench, the kettle boiling. Fifteen feet now, he paused, sure he could hear the boys singing.

'Cheerily marching to battle, cheerily singing our song.'

I'm coming lads. Ten feet to go and he raised his head, now able to see the sandbags on the trench lid ahead, and he joined in with the song.

'Leeds boys are we, gallant and free, in duty and daring strong!'

The earth shook and his fingers were within touching distance of the bags. Summoning all his strength, Arthur raised his arms and pulled himself upright, dragging his legs over the lip of the trench and tumbling down onto the duckboards, the thick mud breaking his fall.

He sat up and looked around. The trench was deserted.

'Lads, where are you? Wilson are you here?'

He paused to catch his breath but almost immediately felt the rats crawling on his legs, under his Greatcoat, trying to find a way in. He set off crawling along the trench, through the mud and the shit and the blood, and eventually he spotted the glow of a fire, a group of men huddled around it, their heads covered by blankets and only their dark eyes visible.

'Lads I'm here. I made it.'

None of the men turned round, they all kept staring into the flickering light of the fire.

'I made it. I'm safe.'

Arthur dragged himself forward and reached out to touch the shoulder of the first soldier. The man turned and the blanket slipped back to reveal a face destroyed by putrefaction. The left eye bulged from its socket and the cheek was missing, maggots swarming in the gums above exposed teeth.

Arthur recoiled in horror and the man spoke in German and turned back to the fire.

The other men turned to look in his direction now and he noticed the uniforms, the helmets, the wounds, the missing limbs.

'You're German.'

'We're dead.' Replied the boy with the blond hair and the prominent ears. He grinned, white teeth between thin lips and a large hole in his stomach.

'He's come for you.' The boy pointed over Arthur's shoulder and he turned to see the dog, head low and ears flat, baring its teeth.

Arthur tried to scream for help but the words wouldn't come and the dog approached, its bark deep and threatening.

Arthur cried out as the hand touched his shoulder. The dog was still barking and he opened his eyes, his heart pounding and gasping for breath.

"Are you alright lad? I think you nodded off and were having a nightmare."

Arthur struggled to his feet, his hands shaking uncontrollably as he stood before the old park keeper.

"I think I fell asleep." The dog was still barking, its owner kicking a ball for it near the Holbeck Moor bandstand.

The park keeper smiled. "Yes I was watching you. I thought you were going to tumble off the bench at one point."

Arthur shuffled and looked down at his feet.

"I see you here most days. You were in the Pals weren't you? I suppose you were there on the first?"

Arthur nodded and looked away, watching the pigeons swoop low over the turrets of the Union Workhouse. The old man nodded and smiled, reaching out to touch Arthur's arm, then pausing as Arthur flinched.

"There's no law against having a kip on the moor lad, you can have a nap on that bench whenever you want, just don't catch a chill in this cold." The park keeper removed his cap and Arthur muttered a thank you and turned to leave.

"And don't worry, better dreams will come in time, I'm sure of it." The old man shouted after him, but Arthur didn't look back as he shuffled away, shoulders hunched and cap pulled low over his eyes. He was still shaking as he took the long path, round the other side of the bandstand, away from the barking of the dog which he knew he'd still hear, long after he'd left the moor.

Chapter 21

"There is no other option George. I'm sorry, but there's simply no other way." Joseph O'Connell hadn't even bothered to remove his hat. He'd rehearsed the delivery of his ultimatum in front of the mirror three times and anticipated George Cribbins' response. He knew it wasn't going to be an amicable conversation.

"But you're destroying my life Joe! To say I'd suffered a nervous breakdown and was unaware of what I was doing when I made those payments is going to make me unemployable again as a teacher, you must see that?" Cribbins struggled to maintain his composure as he slumped back in his chair, across the desk from O'Connell.

"What are the other choices George? You were the club's Chief Financial Officer when illegal payments were made to players. Admitting that you understood what you were doing would see you jailed, then you would certainly struggle for future employment as an educator..."

"Jail? I never intended to break the law..."

"Corruption George. That's how it would be viewed. And during a national crisis too. I would imagine the courts would take a very dim view of such activity."

"I can't do it Joe. I'm not going to knowingly ruin my life, I can't." Cribbins' lip trembled and his hands shook visibly.

"I don't want to sound over dramatic George, but the potential legal consequences are probably the least of your concerns." O'Connell stepped forward and rested both hands on the desk, his bushy white eyebrows framing an uncompromising stare.

"As I've mentioned before, Mr. Holleran's involvement in the club's affairs was based on certain guarantees. Those being that his assistance would be kept very much in the background. He's made it clear to me that he will take a very dim view of his business affairs being discussed in the public domain...a VERY dim view. And with Mr Holleran, I don't think I need to spell out to you what that is likely to mean."

"Are you threatening me Joe? Is Frank Holleran having me followed?" Cribbins' vague recollection of strangers loitering around the enclosure and late-night motor car headlights shining in his window suddenly took on a more sinister relevance.

O'Connell seemed about to speak, but checked himself and addressed the cowering figure before him in hushed tones.

"George,both you and I are aware of Mr.Holleran's ...reputation. I don't need to threaten you lad. Your own common sense tells you the danger you're in...we're all in, if this mess goes public. Best for everyone if it goes away quickly and quietly. Best for the club too, and I know how much you care about the City."

"I never wanted this, never wanted any of it." Cribbins buried his head in hands and his sobs caused O'Connell to shift uneasily at the other side of the desk.

"I know lad, I know. None of us did. We just wanted the best for the club. But this is the only way. The responsibility has to be yours and yours alone. You'd taken leave of your senses due to the pressure. Temporary insanity. That's your best defence."

"MY best defence?" Cribbins lowered his hands and met O'Connell's uneasy gaze.

"Yes George, yours. The position of myself and the rest of the directors is that we were unaware of any payments made to guest players beyond the permitted travel expenses."

Cribbins shook his head and forced a smile through his tears.

"Fuck you Joseph."

O'Connell ignored the insult. "Delaney is doing what he can with the books. Is there anything else relating to the club's financial affairs that you need to turn over to him?"

Cribbins seemed about to respond but paused.

"I'll need money." He dabbed at his eyes with his knuckle and a new resolve appeared in his eyes.

"Money?"

"Yes George, you're asking me to commit professional suicide, so I'll need compensating. £400 should suffice?"

"£400? Have you taken leave of your senses man? Why would we give you £400 when this whole mess is down to you in the first place?" O'Connell's face flushed purple and he spluttered with laughter."

"£400 and I'll disappear and forget the whole thing."

Still smirking and shaking his head, O'Connell nodded and turned towards the door.

"I'll discuss it with Mr.Holleran, but believe me son, I'm trying to help you. I'm trying to save your life."

Chapter 22

Frank Holleran stumbled along the long, over-heated corridor of Leeds General Infirmary and cursed his crippled foot. His chest felt tight and the red brick walls seemed to be closing in on him as he limped towards the light emanating from a glass panelled door leading to the winter garden facing Great George Street.

He almost collided with two young nurses who bustled past him in the doorway, a fleeting breeze of perfume from their capes a welcome respite from the smell of antiseptic and bleach.

A youth in uniform with a thick bandage covering his eyes was smoking in the doorway and turned, unseeing, as the door slammed shut.

Frank gulped in a lungful of Leeds town centre's sooty air and vainly scanned Great George Street for the car. He removed his pocket watch with a shaking hand. Ten minutes early. Mr Sledge would still be on the Stanningley Road.

He admonished himself for spending so little time with his mother, but he hated hospitals. Hated the smell, the heat, the officialdom. Most of all he hated the fact that his mother was there because of him.

He had enough contacts to have dodged his military service, but back in 1914 when all the lads had headed down to the Pals recruitment office in Swinegate, there was no thought of not going. It was to be a grand adventure, a jolly trip through France, with the chance to have a bash at Fritz, get acquainted with the famous French lasses and maybe even conduct a little business too. 'Don't worry. We'll be home before Spring Mam.'

Of course she hadn't objected. She knew the business and she was a fighter. She'd had to be. To be an unmarried mother was a disgrace, a stain on the family which had pushed her own mother into an early grave, and seen her packed off to an aunts in Wales for the first two years of Frank's life.

Holleran bit his lip at the thought of her in a hospital bed, her hand wrapped in bandages like an Egyptian mummy, the look she'd given him as he'd burst through the doors.

"Who told you?" Was all she'd said.

He'd mumbled an answer. How could he tell her that he'd found out that the Chinese had sent them a warning when he'd found her severed finger on his doormat, gift wrapped with a red ribbon.

His fault. His miscalculation that he still controlled the canal from the Leeds basin to Skipton, even though most of the boys were with him in France; His need to keep the Chinese happy that had led him to guarantee security for their product as it transited West Yorkshire, en-route to Liverpool from Hull; His allegiance with the Folans of Bradford which had ended in the hail of machine gun fire which took down Tommy Folan at Rossignol Wood; His lack of control over his patch, which had led to half a ton of Chinese Opium being stolen from a narrowboat at Apperley Bridge locks. His fault that he wasn't there, that they were now in debt to the Manchester Tong, and had now lost their only certain way of paying them back.

"Fuck. Fuck." Frank muttered and shook his head, causing the blind soldier to turn towards him and smile.

"Everything okay friend?"

"Fine." Frank pushed a packet of Woodbines into the soldier's jacket pocket as he spotted the car turn into Great George Street and began to limp down the steps.

Mr Sledge had opened the passenger side door and his grandfather was on the pavement before he'd reached the street.

"How is she?"

Frank nodded. "She's tough. Not saying much. They grabbed her from behind when she left the market, put something over her mouth, she tasted chemicals. Next thing she knew she woke up in an alley off Kirkgate covered in blood."

"I'll need the names." His grandfather looked beyond him to the hospital building.

"Names? Whose names?"

"These Manchester Chinese. The ones we owe."

Frank shook his head. "Leave this to me, it's my problem Grandad..."

The old man turned and looked him up and down.

"Sorting it out your way has landed us where we are. Write down some names, the leaders, I'll resolve this situation my way, to at least buy us some more time."

"Your way?" Frank watched as the old man set off walking slowly through the hospital garden.

"Yes my way. The old way. Give Mr. Sledge the names Frank, then get on with running your business while I go and see my daughter."

Chapter 23

Charlie Cookson winced in pain as he daubed a thumbful of antiseptic on an inch long cut above his left eyebrow. The smiling face of Harry Millership appeared behind him in the cracked mirror of the Elland Road changing room.

"Rough old bugger that Walden, isn't he?"

Cookson nodded. "Caught me with his elbow when the ball was down the other end of the field. He who laughs last though eh Taff?"

"Too right Charlie, you hit him like an express train! Went down like a sack of spuds he did!"

Cookson straightened his tie and turned away from the mirror, leaving the way clear for Millership to begin straightening his own collar.

He folded his damp towel and stuffed it into a blue duffle bag, then reached to the peg for his overcoat.

"Charlie, your presence is required in the boardroom!" A disembodied voice shouted from the half-open changing room door.

"By who?" Cookson's question went unanswered, prompting Millership to catch his eyes in the mirror.

"Pay rise Charlie. Has to be. Or maybe an England call up for when the internationals start again."

"More likely a fine for that tackle." Both men laughed as Cookson picked up his bag and headed through the door, along the corridor where Old Ned the groundsman was extracting himself from a pair of muddy wellies, up the wooden staircase with its mildew-stained wallpaper and a framed painting of past City benefactor Norris Hepworth.

The boardroom door was ajar, over-emphasing the transition from bare floorboards to fraying purple carpet. The smell of cigar smoke old and new was evident as he pushed open the door to be greeted by the furrowed brow of Frank Holleran.

Cookson nodded a greeting and Holleran responded with a flick of his index finger to tell Cookson to close the door.

"Sit down Charlie." A cigar burned in a brass ashtray on the mahogany table and Holleran leant forward and retrieved it, flicked off a tail of ash and narrowed his eyes as his inhalation caused the tip to glow orange.

Cookson sat, resisting the urge to dab at his forehead, which he suspected was starting to bleed.

"I have a proposition for you, relating to our previous discussion." Holleran's steady gaze remained on the cigar as he spoke.

"But you know what happened to Percy? I wrote to him as you asked but I found out about his injury a few days later. I'm sorry, but I did what you asked..."

"Where is he now?" Holleran tilted the cigar and watched the smoke curl upwards in front of him.

"He's convalescing in Hampshire, I haven't seen him. He's not well enough to travel north yet."

"Got his 'W' stripe though didn't he? Losing both legs will be classed as 100% disability, what's that, forty shillings a week?"

"I..I don't know about that. I hope he'll be looked after, but I don't know..."

"But he's a deserter Charlie!" Holleran sat back and drew on the cigar, his eyes now fixed on Cookson.

"So you say..."

"So I say." Holleran smiled. "Not just me though. Most of the lads in the battalion knew that we'd scarpered. We talked about it for weeks before we skipped it. Asked a few of them to join us but they got the wind up at the last minute. And our sergeant knew, he just couldn't prove it."

"But you'll incriminate yourself if you spill the beans about Percy. You'll lose your own pension." Cookson lowered his voice, glancing back towards the door.

"Lose my 10%, Class 5 pension eh? Six shillings per week..I spend that on a good meal at Powolny's." Holleran laughed.

"You'd be prosecuted though?"

"Maybe. Maybe not. The Red Tops tend to be lenient with offenders who see the error of their ways and turn in themselves and others. And my mother doesn't pride herself on having a war hero for a son. She sees the whole bloody debacle for the sham it was." Holleran leant forward and balanced the cigar on the rim of the ash tray.

"The fact is Charlie, if our activities in France come to light, the impact on my life will be negligible. For poor, crippled Percy, it will be devastating. He'll be resigned to a life on the pavement outside the Pygmalion with a begging bowl once he gets out of the glasshouse. You're bleeding."

Charlie Cookson removed a handkerchief from his coat pocket and dabbed at his forehead.

"So what do you want from me?"

"I need you to do a job for me. A very important job."

"I never joined up, I've never fired a gun..."

"Not that kind of job." Holleran stood up and walked to the window and peered into the darkness.

Cookson's mouth was dry and he felt unable to speak, the silence broken only by the sound of his own breathing. Holleran turned to face him.

"During the war, the ability of our guest players to turn up on a Saturday afternoon was dictated by the vagaries of transport and the unpredictable shift patterns of their employers. As you know, those occasions where our most skillful performers failed to appear, unfortunately led to some unexpected defeats when we were flying high in the season we won the Midland League.

"We started some of those games with nine men."

Holleran smiled. "Most unfortunate. Unless of course, those unexpected defeats weren't actually unexpected, and certain parties were able to take advantage via the betting markets."

"They were your players. You controlled them."

"Not quite. The players are professionals. Upstanding sportsmen. They never wanted to let anyone down. What could they do though if their employer insisted on them working their shift? Or if the driver we arranged for them didn't turn up?"

Holleran reached for the cigar. "I didn't need to control the players. I controlled their employers, and I provided the ways and means for them to travel to Leeds for matches. That was enough."

"You must be the only man in Leeds who isn't overjoyed now the war has ended." Cookson shook his head.

"I did my bit Charlie. Joined up in '14 with the rest of the lads. No slacking here. What about you? What did you do in the war? Kicked a ball around in front of a crowd of old men and young larrikins for four years while the Pals were being cut down in their hundreds."

"I had a contract. The club made it clear that I was expected to fulfil the terms I'd signed up to." Cookson felt his face flush and dabbed at the wound above his eye. "So what is this job you want me to do?"

Holleran slowly lifted the cigar from the ashtray and raised it to his lips, his eyes fixed on Cookson's.

"I have a problem. A debt incurred while I was overseas which now requires urgent settlement. The small gains available from betting on an occasional, unexpected City defeat were fine to keep things ticking over during the war, but this requires something big. Much larger bets laid in London at much higher odds."

"Like what? A cup tie defeat to a lower league team?"

Holleran smiled again as he observed the orange glow at the tip of his cigar.

"There are bookies in London, Chinese mainly, who will offer odds on virtually anything. I even heard a tale of a man who won fifty thousand betting on a race between two wood lice..." Holleran sucked on the cigar. "Anyway, these bookies don't only offer a price on the outcome of the match. You can get odds on virtually anything which could occur during the ninety minutes."

"You're talking about match squaring, pure and simple." Cookson stood, shaking his head. "I think you're talking to the wrong man Mr. Holleran, I won't do it."

"There's good money to be made Charlie, for us both, and your brother."

"George Anderson? You remember him?" Cookson folded his arms and looked across at Holleran.

"Anderson got greedy. Squaring the Manchester-Liverpool Easter game was a stupid risk and it was no surprise he got caught. My associates made that very clear to him..."

"He's still in jail. And the other seven are banned from playing professional football for life. I can't risk that, especially now..." Cookson turned towards the door.

"Then you'd better make contact with Percy and tell him to expect a visit from the red tops. I wonder if they'll make an allowance for him not standing for the judge while he's in the dock, seeing as he has no legs?"

Cookson paused with his hand on the door handle, still facing away from Holleran.

"What is it you want?" he muttered, almost inaudibly.

"Sit down Charlie." Holleran tapped the mahogany desk but Cookson remained standing, slowly turning to face him.

"Just tell me what you want."

Holleran sat back and spoke slowly and deliberately.

"In the game against The Wednesday next week, you will give away two penalties in the last half hour. It doesn't matter how you concede the first, it can be a handball or a foul, but for the second, the offence will be serious foul play, serious enough to see you sent from the pitch."

"I can't do that, how can I..?"

"You're a defender Charlie. It's easy. It's not like I'm asking you to score three goals or something."

Cookson placed his hands on the back of the chair and stared at the desk.

"Is it clear what you have to do?" Holleran raised the cigar to his lips then withdrew it without inhaling.

"If I do this, is that it? It's over then?"

"I can't promise that Charlie. It depends on the odds myself and my associates achieve, how much we manage to wager, a number of variables. It may be that we need your help with future events, it may not. Let's call it an open ended arrangement. If so, you will continue to benefit."

Cookson nodded, chewing his lip, and turned for the door.

"To the Sheffield Wednesday game Charlie. Good luck. And remember I'll be watching, we'll all be watching. And Charlie..."

Cookson paused in the doorway.

"You're still bleeding old pal."

Chapter 24

Arthur Rowley stood in the doorway of the White Horse and watched the orange glow of a tram's lights disappear into a cloud of his own exhaled cigarette smoke. The murmur of voices and tapping of pint pots on wooden tables from the bar behind him were momentarily lost to the whistle of a late train pulling out of Armley station round the corner from the pub.

He rubbed at his eyes which stung in response to the acrid fumes drifting across the rooftops from Blakey's works. He bent to stretch his back. The injury still troubled him, especially after a long shift, and Mrs Holleran was a hard task master, snapping at his heels if he lingered over his tobacco break. Her mood seemed to have darkened further since the accident which had seen her return to the pub with a heavily bandaged right hand, and Arthur sensed a tension between Frank and his mother and grandfather.

The splutter of an engine caused Arthur to turn and look up the hill, to see Mr.Sledge's truck approaching. Instinctively, he ducked back into the shadows of the doorway and tossed his cigarette onto the cobbles.

A muffled cough from the alleyway alongside the pub told Arthur that he hadn't been alone in monitoring the comings and goings of the street, and as the truck door opened he heard the voice of Alston Holleran.

"How many?"

"Five. All male and less than a year old." Eldon Sledge stepped from the truck and reached into the back, to emerge with a hessian sack which he handed to the old man.

Arthur leant back in the shadows and tried to slow his breathing as he struggled to hear the mens' conversation.

"Is everything in order for tomorrow?"

Yes, I've been across to Manchester. Checked the location. Everything looks straight forward."

"You have the chemicals?"

"Everything is ready."

"Okay Mr.Sledge. Be very careful. This can't be traced back to us or the suffering we're experiencing now will pale into insignificance. And not a word to my grandson."

"I understand." Mr. Sledge climbed back into the truck and the engine rattled into life as Alston Holleran dragged the sack into the alleyway and Arthur heard a door scrape on the cobbles as it was tugged shut.

Arthur stepped forward and peered into the gloom of the alley which led to the stables at the rear of the pub. A light flickered in an upper window and he thought he could hear the old man cough. He took three steps into the alleyway and scuffed the ground with the end of his boot, then turned and walked back towards Town Street. Arthur stooped in the glow of a gas lamp, and ran his finger across the toe of his boot, as the pub door opened and he heard Kitty Holleran's voice.

"Arthur? Are you out there? There's ash trays need emptying and pots need washing in here. Where are you?"

Arthur didn't answer. He raised his index finger to the light and rubbed at it with his thumb, then lifted it to his nose and sniffed. As he suspected, it was a smell he knew well, a smell he hoped he'd forgotten. The smell of freshly spilled blood.

Chapter 25

George Cribbins closed the door of the tobacconists, and pulled his hat down low until the brim was directly in his eyeline. He ducked his head and stepped onto the wet cobbles of Domestic Street, looking right towards the railway bridge and the tram terminus. Moving quickly, scanning the empty road behind him, past the Methodist chapel and left into Willoughby Grove. Two lines of washing hung forlornly across the street, not recovered before the morning's rain, and now turning grey in Holbeck's soot-tainted breeze. Cribbins nodded to an old woman stooping to donkey-stone her front step. She looked him up and down and scowled. A stare for a slacker, perfected over the last four years.

Cribbins stopped and turned again, looking back to the corner of the street where a young man in a bowler hat stopped to light a cigarette, before casting a glance in his direction as he crossed the road. Cribbins' heart beat faster and he paused, turning again to watch the man move out of sight upon reaching the street corner.

He was sure the man had been behind him as he'd passed the cricket ground on Elland Road. Cribbins tried to recall his walking speed. Had the man increased his pace to keep up with him? The old woman tipped water from an iron pale into the gutter and muttered something as she watched him. Cribbins carried on along the street, catching the movement of net curtains from the corner of his eye. His mouth was dry and his heart beat harder as he reached a blue painted door and knocked, scanning both sides of the street as he did.

The brass knob rattled and the door swang open, the rosy cheeks and bright eyes of Eliza Rowley peered round the door frame, her mousy blond hair cut fashionably short in a bobbed style.

"Hello George, what brings you here?" She smiled and Cribbins had to prevent himself from hurrying over the threshold to escape the prying eyes of the street.

"Good Day Eliza, is Edgar home?" He had one foot on the step and cast a final glance down the terraced street as she opened the door and beckoned him in.

"Edgar! George is here to see you." She called up the stairs and turned smiling, as footsteps thudded on the floorboards above.

"I'll mash some tea. Sit down won't you?" Eliza motioned to a wooden chair beside a small dining table under the window, and Cribbins sat, peering through the net curtains as he did.

Heavy footsteps on the stairs heralded Edgar's arrival, buttoning his waist coat and flattening his pomaded hair.

"To what do we owe this honour George?" He smiled as Cribbins stood to greet him.

"I'm sorry to turn up unannounced Edgar, but I'm going away for a while and I have something for you." Cribbins stood and fumbled in his overcoat to retrieve a manila envelope which he thrust towards his friend.

"Calm down old pal, what's the matter?" Edgar caught his wife's eye in the scullery, and motioned towards the front door with a slight flick of his head.

"We've used our sugar ration again. I'll pop round to Martha's to see if she has some. Her brother was supposed to be getting hold of some ham too, so I might have a treat when I come back." She wiped her hands on her apron and bustled out of the door which she left slightly ajar.

"The door..." Cribbins looked agitated at the sight of the cobbled street beyond the threshold.

"It's fine. What's the matter George? You're a bundle of nerves." Edgar placed the envelope on the table between them and looked into his friend's tear-filled eyes.

"They're after me Edgar. I think they're going to kill me." Cribbins' lip quivered and he removed his hat and nervously flicked at the brim with his thumbs.

"Kill you? Who? Why? Take your time and tell me what's happened."

Cribbins took a deep breath and glanced through the net curtains, then to the open door as he began his tale.

"I told you about the trouble at City. The payments I was told to make to the guest players. The directors are trying to cover it all up, make me take all the blame, say I had a nervous breakdown caused by the stress of running the team while Mr.Chapman was doing his war work. If it comes out, I'll never work again, never get another teaching job Edgar..."

"Then don't do it. Tell the truth."

"I wanted to, but Mr. O'Connell said that we had to keep it quiet. That if there was an official enquiry it would cause big problems with Frank Holleran. Then I started to notice things. Men I'd never seen before hanging around outside the ground. Sometimes a motor car would pull up outside the house at night, shining the headlamps into the room. I could see the shadow of someone in the driver's seat watching me. People following me. I'm sure a chap followed me here just now." Cribbins glanced again at the half open door.

"So what will you do? What's this?" Edgar nodded at the envelope on the table.

"They made me hand over all the accounting records and bank statements and the cheque book with the payment stubs showing amounts paid to the players. They paid me a month's wages on condition that I sign an agreement not to speak about the club's affairs during the war, a confidentiality clause."

"Oh George..." Edgar shook his head and pointed towards the envelope on the table. "And this?"

"I didn't give them everything. I made some of the payments from my own bank account and the cheque stubs are in there. I also kept a duplicate set of ledgers – I was scared of the stand catching fire so I always had copies at home. There are also some telegrams from Mr.O'Connell regarding the arrangements Mr.Holleran had made with some of the players, how much to pay them and the like..."

"So there's your proof! That you weren't acting alone. That the directors knew that payments were being made and that Holleran was acting as an unlicenced agent for City. Do you want me to write this up for the Post?"

"No! No Edgar, that's not why I've given it to you. If the information becomes public, I'm pretty certain you'll find me at the bottom of the canal. Holleran will see to that. This is my insurance policy. I'll let it be known that there are other documents retained in a safe place, and if anything were to happen to me, they would be made public."

Edgar nodded. "I understand, don't worry, I'll keep them safe, but you have to stay in contact so I know you're safe. Where will you go?"

Before Cribbins could answer, both men turned at the sound of the front door hinge creaking.

"Is that you 'Liza?" Edgar's question got no response and he stood slowly. "Maybe just the wind."

A louder creak preceded the door swinging slowly open and the pale, unshaven, hollow-eyed face of Arthur Rowley appeared around the doorframe.

"Arthur, you gave us a turn."

"Sorry... Mr.Cribbins." Arthur nodded and mumbled a greeting then shuffled through the room and straight up the stairs.

"Where will you go George?" Edgar turned back to his friend who replaced his hat and extended his hand.

"Better you don't know Edgar. I'll stay in touch."

"Stay safe old pal." Edgar Rowley held the door open then watched his friend pull his hat low over his eyes and hurry along the damp flagstones of Willoughby Grove, turning with a fleeting half-wave before disappearing behind a washing line of grey laundry.

Chapter 26

Frank Holleran looked into the large brass mirror behind the reception desk of Briggate's Grand Central Hotel and straightened his tie. He removed his hat and flatted his hair and smiled at the concierge.

"This way sir. Mr.Dingyuan is in the restaurant." The concierge extended his arm to direct Holleran, who swallowed hard and rubbed his hands on his trousers, trying to rid them of moisture ahead of an anticipated handshake with Ti Xi Dingyuan. Important that he showed no fear. No sign of nerves at being summoned to a face to face meeting with the leader of the Manchester Tong. Not intimidated by the reputation of the head man of the Northern Tiandihui, Three Harmonies Triad, the Who Shing Wo Black Society, to whom he owed a six figure sum.

Holleran stumbled on the thick pile of the carpet as the concierge led him past the two Chinamen seated in reception; through the dining room, past the old ladies from Headingley sipping their afternoon tea with flu masks suspended beneath their chins; past the Jewish doctors from Chapeltown, heads dipped in quiet conference; past the pianist, eyes closed, robotically plinking away at Brahms Little Sandman; past the obese businessman contemplating a whole roast chicken with lust-filled eyes. To the corner of the room. A small man in a dark suit, a tall black hat on the white tablecloth before him.

"Mr.Dingyuan, your guest, sir." The concierge smiled and Frank Holleran extended his hand.

Ti Xi tilted his tea cup in its saucer and didn't look up.

"Sit." His voice almost a whisper, he waited for Frank Holleran to sit opposite him before raising his eyes.

"Tea, Mr. Holleran?"

Frank nodded and Ti Xi reached across to lift a silver tea pot, allowing Holleran to observe him more closely.

An unlined brown face aged him anywhere between fifty and seventy, brown monolid eyes, a button nose above a drooping, wispy moustache. His hair too black for his age, pulled into a long plait extending down his back.

Frank Holleran took a breath and faced the man who had arranged for the amputation of his mother's finger, and then posted the severed digit to him.

"Ti Xi, I'm doing everything in my power to pay back what I owe for your lost produce. I don't need any further reminders. My inside man, the Leeds City player, will ensure our bets deliver on Saturday. I hope you have sufficient funds wagered to cover the debt."

Holleran picked up his tea cup and took a sip. Ti Xi gazed into his eyes, his expression betraying neither happiness or anger, and an awkward silence descended, broken only by the sounds of low chatter and cutlery scraping on plates.

"I'm as frustrated as you are by the delays we've had in either locating the missing produce or compensating you..."

"That's not why I'm here." Ti Xi's voice remained low, barely audible above the sounds of the dining room.

"I'm sorry? I assumed..."

"That's not the reason I asked you to come here today Mr.Holleran. That matter is purely business, this is more important." Ti Xi's left eye flickered and his nostrils flared, causing Holleran to detect a suppression of explosive anger. He raised his eyebrows, half not wanting to know the real reason for the meeting.

Ti Xi looked down at his tea cup, then quickly back to Holleran, his eyes probing for signs of distress or fear.

"My grandson." He began slowly. "My grandson is missing. He never came home from school on Tuesday."

Frank Holleran felt a rivulet of sweat in the small of his back and an itch above his right eyebrow, but he remained still, frozen, struggling to control a shake in the hand which held his tea cup.

"Your grandson? You think I had something to do with that?" Holleran felt a tremor in his voice but couldn't tell whether it was driven by terror or his own rage.

"I don't think that Mr.Holleran. If I really thought that, you would already be dead, as would all your family." Ti Xi remained impassive, but the look in his eyes alerted Holleran to the lethal potential of the situation.

"Then why are you here, in Leeds?"

"I have many enemies Mr.Holleran. Here in your city, in Liverpool, Sheffield, Hull. My daughter and her husband are beside themselves with worry. I must do all I can to find the boy, leave no stone unturned in questioning those who may want to hurt me by harming my family. The boy is eleven. Maybe, I hope, he is simply away on some childish adventure with his friends..."

"I'm sure that's the case Ti Xi, boys of that age get up to all sorts of capers, maybe they've gone off camping..." Holleran was eager to look on the bright side.

"If however, Mr. Holleran, I find that the boy has been abducted by a business rival, then I will unleash a fury never before seen in this country or any other. We are Hongmen, for us, honour and the obeyance of rules are of the utmost importance. If those rules are broken, then our Boo-how-doy, our soldiers, will go to war. And it will be a most terrible war, Mr.Holleran."

"Let's look on the bright side hey? I'm sure the lad will turn up safe, and in the meantime, I'll put out the word around Leeds to keep an eye out for youngsters camping in the fields out towards Wharfedale, in case they're heading for the Yorkshire Dales." Holleran smiled but Ti Xi's face remained impassive.

"Regarding the Leeds-Sheffield game...I trust you wagered enough to recoup the loss of the produce?" Frank drained his tea cup and replaced it in the saucer.

"On that subject," Ti Xi spoke slowly in his barely audible whisper, causing Frank to lean in towards him. "You'll be pleased to know that I have regained possession of the opium. Representatives of the men who stole it made the great mistake of trying to sell it on to some of my associates in Liverpool. They suffered the consequences of their miscalculation."

"That's splendid news Ti Xi," Holleran beamed across the table. "Does that mean..."

"It has no impact on your situation. You lost my produce, and you must repay me, Mr. Holleran. I hope for your sake that your footballer does what's required on Saturday. Now if you will excuse me, I need to continue my journey to try and locate my grandson. His name is Li Yuan, and I will find him. You can contact me by telephone on this number if you obtain any information."

Ti Xi Dingyuan placed a slip of paper on the white table cloth. He then picked up his tall black hat and positioned it on his head, and stared hard into Frank Holleran's eyes.

"And remember my words, Mr.Holleran. If anyone has harmed my grandson, I will unleash a war unlike anything you have ever experienced before. I hope very much for your sake you have no involvement in his disappearance."

Chapter 27

Frank Holleran gripped the steering wheel which shook violently as the car negotiated the cobbles of Armley Town Street. He cursed a slow-moving beer dray attempting to make a left turn from Carr Crofts, and swerved to a stop outside the White Horse. Slamming the door shut, he dashed past the old poacher exiting the tap room with his sack of fresh rabbits, up the steps into the pub, blinking in the smoke of early afternoon drinkers.

Arthur Rowley was washing ash trays behind the bar and looked up as Frank appeared, breathless and perspiring.

"Arthur, have you seen my grandad?"

Arthur raised a hand towards the rear door of the pub and Frank was gone before he could speak.

"Frank? Frank? What's the matter?" Kitty Holleran emerged from the saloon bar and followed her son towards the door.

Emerging into the yard alongside the pub, Frank headed to the open door of an outhouse from where he could hear the muffled voices of his grandfather and Mr Sledge.

"Grandad! Grandad!" Frank stormed towards the building with his mother following in his wake.

"Frank! What's the matter?"

Frank turned and shook his head, his face contorted with rage and seemingly unable to speak.

The outhouse door opened to reveal Alston Holleran and Eldon Sledge, each removing a soiled overall, and Frank turned to face his grandfather.

"Tell me you haven't...please tell me you're not involved."

"Involved in what? What's he talking about dad?" Kitty Holleran stood, hands on hips, scowling at the three men.

Alston Holleran wiped his hands on the folded overall and shrugged.

"It had to be done. We needed better protection."

"No! No! Fucking Hell, no!" Frank Holleran sank to his knees, his head in his hands.

"What? What's happened? Dad, what have you done?"

Alston Holleran looked from his grandson to his daughter as Mr.Sledge nervously shuffled his feet.

"Tell her! Tell her what you did...you stupid, stupid old bastard."

"Frank! Don't ever speak to your grandfather in that way. I'm surprised at you..." Kitty turned to her father and raised her eyebrows, inviting an explanation.

"We needed a more powerful charm. We were in danger, Clem warned me."

"Oh God, what have you done?" It was now Kitty Holleran's turn to raise her heavily bandaged hand to her face as Frank stood up to face his grandfather.

"Go on, tell her. Tell her what you did...I assume you're involved in this too?" Frank looked towards Mr.Sledge who stared at his own shuffling feet.

Frank swallowed hard and took his mother's hand.

"Your father, my grandfather, has killed a child. Killed a little boy because a fucking dog in a dream told him to."

"What? No! Dad, tell me that isn't true...you tell me now!" Kitty broke away and gripped her fathers arm with her unbandaged hand, staring into his eyes.

"Clem isn't a dog. The dog is just his earthly familiar..."The old man raised his voice to address his grandson over his daughter's shoulder.

"Forget ruddy Clem! I don't care whether he's a dog or the devil, what did you do?" Kitty tightened her grip on her father's arm.

"Mr.Sledge apprehended the boy as he left school. Chloroform on a rag, then bundled him into the van and back over the Pennines."

"Oh sweet Jesus no, you didn't...you couldn't." Kitty Holleran began to shake and her eyes prickled with tears.

"Didn't what? Kill him? Of course I didn't. He's alive. We're just...using him, until the danger subsides. Until Frank has fixed his football game to pay back the debt."

"Using him? I don't believe this, I'm going to fucking kill you." Frank Holleran stepped forward but was pushed back by his mother and restrained by Mr.Sledge.

"Using him for what Dad? Where is this boy?" Kitty prodded her father in the chest.

"It's best you don't know. He's sedated, he's fine, we've wrapped him up warm and he has food and water."

"But what are you doing with him? Who is he?" Kitty's face was flushed, and she struggled to hold back from striking her father herself.

"We needed a charm to work against the forces threatening us. The male bloodline is key to negating their power and he's the youngest heir. His blood can be used against them."

"Oh sweet Jesus, not the Chinese." Kitty Holleran looked at her bandaged hand and closed her eyes.

"Can you believe this?" Frank shook his head. "We've indulged him too long with his bloody magic mumbo jumbo. Selling animal hearts pierced with iron to old women who think they'll keep their sons safe in France is one thing, but kidnapping a child and extracting his blood is quite something else."

"It's not mumbo jumbo." The old man stuck out his chin and raised his voice. "You were safe today when you went to meet the Chinaman, why do you think that was?"

"Probably because we met in the dining room of the Grand Central and had agreed it would be just the two of us there, and no weapons."

His grandfather was shaking his head and smiling before Frank had finished speaking.

"Look in the top pocket of your overcoat."

Frank grimaced and felt in his pocket to produce a square of hessian sack bound with a purple ribbon.

"What the hell is this?" Frank began to untie the bundle.

"Don't open it! Keep it secured with a four-sided bow or it will lose its power."

"Its power! Have you listened to yourself? I'm sick and tired of this nonsense, taking orders from an imaginary dog." Frank tossed the package onto the cobbles.

"This boy then..."Kitty Holleran stood between her father and son. "You haven't said exactly who he is."

113

Frank began to laugh quietly to himself and looked at his grandad.

"Do you want to tell her or should I? That's the best bit mum, these two fools have only kidnapped the grandson of the headman of the Manchester Tiandihui, the Chinese Black Society!"

"Ti Xi's grandson? Oh God Dad, what have you done?

"Signed our death warrant, that's what he's done." Frank stared at his grandfather.

"No, no. The boy has been blindfolded, he hasn't seen us. Once the debt is paid off this Saturday, Mr.Sledge can take him up onto the moors by the Huddersfield road and let him go. They'll never know it was us." Alston Holleran looked at Mr.Sledge and received a vigorous nod of affirmation.

Kitty Holleran broke the ensuing silence with a long intake of breath.

"That's a risk though. What if he heard something that could lead them here? A train whistle from the station, a beer delivery... I don't know..."

"What other choice do we have though?" Frank kicked at the cobbles beneath his feet and the question hung ominously between the four of them, each trying to dispel an obvious solution that none wanted to contemplate.

The metallic clank of a bucket tumbling down three steps broke the silence.

"I'm sorry, I didn't see it." Arthur Rowley stammered as he stooped to retrieve the pail. "The Drayman's here Mrs.Holleran. Asking for you."

Kitty Holleran turned and walked towards him.

"How long were you stood there Arthur?" Frank Holleran called as Arthur set off up the steps ahead of her.

"Beg your pardon Mr Holleran?" Arthur stopped, his eyes flicking nervously.

"Nothing Arthur." Frank looked away, avoiding the gaze of his grandfather and Mr.Sledge. "You carry on lad."

Chapter 28

Edgar Rowley knew something was wrong as he turned the corner from Domestic Street into Willoughby Grove and spotted Eliza, still in her munitions overalls and bonnet, standing on the step of their terraced house.

"What's the matter?" he mouthed from a hundred yards away and his wife shook her head and beckoned him to hurry, before pushing open the front door and disappearing up the steps.

"What is it? What's the matter?" Edgar removed his hat and hung it on the peg behind the door and began to remove his overcoat as his wife entered the scullery in silence.

Edgar followed her into the small room with its Yorkshire flagstone floor and two seater table, upon which was resting a small square parcel wrapped in a section of hessian sack. Two loops of ribbon which had secured the parcel lay on the table alongside it.

"What's that?" Edgar approached the bundle and recoiled upon tugging it open.

"You tell me." Eliza had a hand over her mouth and her face was pale.

"Where did you find it?"

Eliza sighed and tapped her fingers on the cooking range.

"You know we've been noticing a lot of flies for the time of year?"

Edgar nodded, his brow furrowed.

Well, I never go into Arthur's room, but when I got back from work, I could hear a buzzing from there. When I looked there were two big bluebottles on the window...and a strange smell."

Edgar stepped forward again and tugged open the parcel to reveal a blackened section of flesh, pierced by a dozen nails.

"My God." Edgar recoiled. "Where did you find this?"

"It was under his bed, beneath the headboard. What do you think it is?"

"Based on my discussions with Cliff, my guess is that it's a section of heart...the heart of an animal..I hope."

Edgar and Eliza looked from each other to the piece of rotting flesh on their table.

"The Beast Slayer attacks...why would Arthur do such a thing?" Edgar rubbed at his forehead with both hands. "I just don't understand."

"That's not all." He looked up to see Eliza holding a white envelope. "This was under his pillow."

Edgar took the envelope and removed from it a fragile, yellowed piece of parchment, covered in a black scrawl of handwritten verse.

"What is this?"

"Read it." Eliza pulled a wooden chair from under the table and sat down as Edgar began to read aloud.

Kings and slaves, to my keen eye, their future prophesies supply.

For all the stars that at our birth, are set to rule our fate on earth.

I shall interpret, and set right, translate the language of the night.

Descended from a line of seers, Wisemen for two hundred years.

Rare my gifts the sick to cure. Health, love, and fortune to ensure.

From birth this calling which is mine, to call upon this art divine.

To own its use, its power feel, and prove indeed that it is real.

From your sick bed, to raise I'll try, while others say "but he must die."

I sense your darkness, feel your pains, and through this charm my power reigns,

It will relieve, revive, restore, my spell will own you ever more.

Edgar folded the paper and replaced it in the envelope as Eliza watched in silence.

"What do you make of it?" She asked eventually,

"It's obviously a spell of some sort. Remember Arthur told us the old man at the White Horse was helping him? I wonder if we've found our infamous Beast Slayer?"

"What will you do? Go to the police?"

Edgar began to fold the edges of the sacking around the heart and pulled the string tight.

"I can't risk that. We don't know what Arthur's involvement is and anyway, how will he react if he thinks we've been snooping in his room?"

"I wasn't snooping Edgar, this is my home!" Eliza snapped at her husband and turned away.

"I know love, I'm sorry. Sorry he's here at all sometimes..." As soon as the words had left his mouth Edgar's face fell and tears filled his eyes.

"Don't..." Eliza wrapped her arms around his neck and pulled him close. "The war is over now. Things will begin to get better for all of us, I'm sure of it."

Edgar buried his face in her neck, tasting the salt of his own tears. "I really hope so Eliza, I do, but at the moment it just feels like everything is getting even worse."

Chapter 29

Although it was a Saturday, Edgar Rowley was awake before first light, and lay in his bed pondering the discovery of the previous day. He'd heard Arthur return from the White Horse at midnight and go to his room, where Edgar had replaced the spell and beast-heart parcel. He'd heard nothing until Arthur had risen at 2am and as usual, spent three hours downstairs, pacing and muttering, before returning to bed before dawn. Eliza's slow breathing told Edgar she was still asleep, and he slipped from beneath the blankets and pulled a dressing gown over his night shirt and crept downstairs.

He put the kettle on and heard the clip-clop of hooves on the cobbles and opened the door to greet Mr.Carr, the milkman.

"Morning Edgar, looking forward to the match today? The Wednesday will be out for revenge after losing the game at Hillsbrough."

"You're right there Mr.Carr, and we had Willis Walker in goal last week but he's not available today. Cook isn't as strong up against the rougher forwards, so that might be a problem for us." Edgar took two pint bottles from a crate Carr was holding.

"Should be a good crowd. More than the 7,000 against Bradford the other week?"

"The club will certainly be hoping so, Mr.Carr, although I think the free entry for wounded soldiers has helped bump up the number. Anyway, let's keep our fingers crossed for the right result and a good turnout of spectators!" Edgar's forced good humour was in sharp contrast to the dark clouds that seemed to hang over the house. He closed the door and entered the scullery, then placed some lard into a frying pan and retrieved three slices of bacon from the cold stone in the larder, then dropped them into the sizzling fat. He peered out of the window, above the chimney pots of the houses opposite, at a leaden grey sky, and tried to decide whether the dark clouds indicated likely rain or that the boiler furnace at Ingram's factory had just been lit.

The first spots began just before midday and persisted as a steady drizzle as Edgar made his way through the warren of redbrick terraces, head down and flat cap pulled down low, so the brim kept the rain from his eyes. He turned up the collar of his coat, glad that he'd opted for his Mackintosh as he crossed Shafton Lane and made his way through the Rydals, the Runswicks and the Recreations. Groves, Streets, Terraces and Places, uniform in appearance with black doorsteps, mahogany doors and white framed windows, the interior view obscured by pristine, white net curtains.

An icy blast of wind made Edgar's eyes water and reminded hm that Christmas was only three weeks away, as he rounded the corner from Crosby Road and turned into Elland Road, with the shrill blast of a whistle at Neville's Engineering works signalling the end of the morning shift. Passing the factory gates, Edgar glanced right to see the first teenage girls, still in grimy overalls, dashing from the main building, wage packets clutched in their hands. For them it would be a hurried visit to the public baths then home to put on their finery, then into town for the Saturday afternoon Bond Street 'crawl'.

Edgar liked to get to the stadium in good time, in order to enjoy the matchday atmosphere, and with over an hour left to kick off, crowds were starting to gather outside the New Peacock pub, with football spectators being joined by workers from the adjoining Barons Close Brick Works on their lunch break. Hawkers lined the route to the enclosure, although the pie and peas generally on offer before the war had disappeared three years earlier as the meat shortage had started to have an impact. Even the Bovril now seemed thin and watery and could only be distinguished from the tea with difficulty.

A steady procession of trams clanked past, seats full and passengers forced to stand shivering on the front gallery above advertising notices for Batty's Nabob Pickles, McCalls Ox Tongues and the current show at the Empire Theatre. A gaggle of grimy faced children stood at the junction of Hoxton Terrace and watched as the spectators passed, the loud chatter and laughter of the strangers a welcome fortnightly distraction from their normal playtime. Edgar walked the length of the uncovered popular stand and around the Wortley End to arrive at a parking area for motor cars in the shadow of the main stand. He passed a group of youngsters admiring Joe O'Connell's Humerette and Jack Whiteman's Wolseley Tourer, and headed for the main entrance. Even after two years, he still got a rush of excitement from flashing his Yorkshire Evening Post press card to be admitted through the directors' entrance door by old Ned, who supplemented his groundsman duties with a matchday job as commissionaire and chief steward.

As usual, Edgar was the first of the reporters to take his seat, with Murdoch of the Mercury and Hanson of the Yorkshire Post propping up the director's bar until just before kick off. Edgar watched as the enclosure began to fill up. The YEP had curtailed its football coverage when the war started and Jack Ebor, its fulltime Sports reporter had joined up. Arguments had raged about whether sport should continue at all, and in the early months of the war, the Post had taken the side of those who felt that continuing to play football was cowardly and unpatriotic. As City continued to play in the Midland League, the local paper had made a conscious effort to look the other way. At best, results were tucked away deep inside the paper, and no details of the match were reported. As it became clear that the war was likely to drag on for many years, the paper's stance had softened, and with no regular sports reporter on the staff, keen City fan Edgar had been an obvious choice to step into the breach.

Things had certainly changed during the last two years. City had risen from a mid ranking 2nd division side to the winners of the Midland championship for the previous two seasons. Off the pitch however, the Elland Road ground was in its usual state of advanced dilapidation, and Edgar cast a wary glance up to the leaking roof of the main stand as the rain began to fall more heavily. The demographic of the spectators had certainly shifted too. At the start of the war, the stands had been an uneasy mix of hard-bitten old men and school aged boys sporting their rosettes and favours in club colours. Now, scanning the crowd in the popular stand, it seemed that the vast majority were wearing either the blue overalls of the munitions factories or the khaki of the forces, home on leave or permanently de-mobbed in recent weeks.

The wounded were now granted free entry, and the cinder track in front of the white picket fence bordering the stands was lined with an unending row of bath chairs. Their more fortunate occupants were those who had managed to escape with the loss of only one leg. In front of the bath chairs lay a number of stretchers, tilted with the help of a stack of bricks, or supported by mates to enable the occupants to view the pitch.

Loud applause and the blowing of tin whistles signified the appearance of the teams onto the muddy enclosure, and Edgar felt a nudge on his arm as Murdoch and Hanson appeared, cigarettes dangling from their lips and smelling of ale.

"Afternoon Rowley, have you seen the team sheet?" Murdoch thrust a type written piece of paper into his hands, with several names scored out and replaced in blue ink.

"Any surprises?" Edgar scanned the sheet and received an immediate appraisal from Hanson.

"Walter Cook in goal for Willis Walker. Tom Cawley in place of Billy McLeod at Outside-Right. Tommy Lamph at Left-Half and Albert McLachlan moving to Right-Half."

"What's this change?" Edgar held the sheet up and peered at a hand written name alongside a scored out typed one.

"Billy Hampson in defence."

"Who's that in place of?"

"Charlie Cookson. No one seems to know where he is."

Chapter 30

"Play up City!" Jack Whiteman was always over excitable at matches and Joseph O'Connell had drawn the short straw amongst the directors in having to sit next to him on the wooden seats of the Elland Road Main Stand. O'Connell grimaced as Whiteman barged into him and stood, arms raised, encouraging his team on against their South Yorkshire rivals.

O'Connell straightened his bowler hat and reached into his overcoat pocket for his cigar case. Tommy Lamph played the ball forward and O'Connell leant forward to keep track of it as it disappeared behind a thick iron stanchion.

A sudden, forceful shove on his shoulder caused him to turn, to be greeted by the reddened, perspiring face of Frank Holleran, leaning across two row of seats to reach him. Holleran's dark eyes flashed with rage and he seemed unable to speak.

"Frank? What's the matter?" O'Connell struggled to turn in his seat beside the standing figure of Whiteman.

"Joe, we need to talk. Now!" Holleran nodded towards the stairs leading to the interior of the stand and turned on his heels before disappearing into the dimly lit recess.

O'Connell stood and pushed his way past the knees of the other directors, muttering his apologies as he made his way along the row, turning in response to a roar from the popular side to see Tom Hall hook a shot above The Wednesday's bar. He gripped the wooden handrail and slowly made his way down the steps into the dimly gaslit corridor leading to the boardroom.

Frank Holleran was waiting, pacing, agitated and obviously furious.

"Frank...what's the..." O'Connell smiled in a futile attempt to diffuse the situation, but his words were lost in a fusillade of prophanities.

"What the fuck is going on Joe? Where is fucking Cookson? Why isn't he in the team?"

O'Connell took a step back and stammered a response.

"What? Frank...Cookson? I'm sorry, I don't..."

"Charlie Fucking Cookson, Joe? Where is he?" Holleran grabbed hold of O'Connell by the lapels and thrust him against the wood panelling,

"Cookson? I don't understand Frank, please, calm down." O'Connell raised his hands in deference and recoiled under the spray of Holleran's saliva, their noses an inch apart.

"Charlie Cookson isn't in the team and I need to know why. If that fucking clown caretaker or Chapman has left him out..." Holleran's eyes blazed with fury, O'Connell could smell the liquor on his breath.

"No Frank, no. Cribbins is gone. Mr Chapman and I picked the team but if I'm honest, I think his mind is still focused more on the world of commerce than..." O'Connell flinched expecting a punch in the gut as Holleran stepped back but instead, the younger man seemed to regain control of his temper and instead took a deep breath.

"Joe, please help me understand, why is Charlie Cookson not in the team today?" His voice was calmer now and O'Connell straightened his jacket before answering.

"I'm sorry Frank, but he's asked for a transfer. In a letter. Didn't even have the decency to do it face to face."

"Fuck! Fucking shit!" Frank Holleran bent forward, his hands wrapped tightly around the back of his head as O'Connell looked on.

"To be honest Frank, he isn't that skillful a player. I wouldn't get too upset about it."

O'Connell knew he'd said the wrong thing when Holleran quickly rose from the floor and again pinned him to the corridor wall, this time with a single hand around his throat.

"Show me the letter Joe," he snarled, before shoving O'Connell back into his own office.

"Here..." Joseph O'Connell's hand shook uncontrollably as he extended the envelope towards Holleran.

"No address, only a telephone number. Fucking coward. Do we know where he lives?" Holleran snorted with derision as he unfolded the single page letter.

"He lived in lodgings in Morley, so I took the car up there to discuss it face to face, but his landlady said he'd moved out, so I called on the telephone.

"And?" Holleran frowned as he quickly began to read the letter aloud.

Dear Mr. O'Connell , As you are aware, my personal circumstances have recently been impacted by a serious injury sustained by my brother Percy on the battlefields of France. As a result, I now find myself the sole financial provider for my brother, and the terms of my current contract with Leeds City do not provide adequate remuneration for my fiscal responsibilities. I have been approached by a number of clubs in the south and midlands offering much improved terms and therefore formally request a transfer from Leeds City and the annulment of my current contract."

"Bloody preposterous. Never heard anything like it. He's on three quid a week as it stands." O'Connell leaned over Holleran's shoulder. "Anyway, I telephoned him and he said he needs money urgently to pay for his brother's care. I reckon he's had his head turned by some of the London clubs starting up again and throwing cash around. I said he had a contract here and he was leaving over my dead body. That's when he started making threats..."

"I hope you can see fit to release me from my contract to enable me to better provide for my brother who is now severely disabled, having selflessly laid down his health and future prosperity for his country, while others sought to profit from this terrible conflict. Should you deny my request, I will be forced to consider alerting the authorities to certain practices and activities which have taken place at the football club in recent years."

Holleran lowered the letter as O'Connell, anticipating a further enraged outburst, took backward steps to position himself behind his desk.

"What do you think he means by that Frank? Who does he mean, others profiting from the war? Anyway, whatever he thinks, he has no evidence of any payments made to the guest players."

Holleran ignored the question. "I'll take the letter Joe. Let me handle it."

"What will you do Frank? We can't afford to pay him any more than he's already on and in the current climate, no other club is going to pay us a fee for him. He's effectively gone on strike."

Holleran folded the letter and put it in the inside pocket of his overcoat and straightened his hat.

"I'll make him see sense Joe. He'll be back in the team for the Hull game, don't you worry."

Chapter 31

Kitty Holleran pulled up a stool, rested her heavily bandaged hand on a bar table and shivered at the chill breeze blowing through the open pub windows facing onto Armley Town Street. The licensing committee required every available window to be opened at afternoon closing time to reduce the spread of the influenza. She pulled a shawl around her shoulders and shivered at the first hints of an icy Yorkshire winter to come, her nose wrinkling at the fumes from Blakey's factory which were rapidly replacing the usual smells of the Saturday lunchtime trade- Beer, tobacco, sweat and illicit black market foodstuffs.

Kitty absent mindedly tugged at her bandage and wondered what the four-fingered hand would look like beneath the covering, and when the searing pain would begin to subside. Arthur Rowley busied himself behind the bar, rinsing pint pots and cleaning ashtrays with a horse-hair brush.

It seemed a normal Saturday afternoon, at least as normal as any other since the war had started. Kitty's first indication that it was anything but normal came as her son's motor car screeched to a halt outside the pub and Frank burst through the doors, his eyes wild, hat clasped in his hand.

"Mum, get Grandad and Mr.Sledge, quick as you like."

"What? What's the matter Frank? What's happened now?" Kitty and Arthur exchanged puzzled glances as Frank dashed through the bar and up the stairs to his office.

"Arthur, will you go call my father please?" Kitty shouted across the bar and followed her son up the stairs to find the three odds takers and the two clerks hurriedly packing away their pens and ledgers and pulling on their coats and hats.

"What are you doing? It's Saturday afternoon, there's football and racing on..."

"Mr. Holleran told us to close up for the day, and go home." Lizzy Crossland, the ledger clerk, shrugged as she carefully positioned the bonnet on her head and picked up her handbag.

Kitty Holleran shook her head and hurried into Frank's small office. He looked up as she entered, two Enfield pistols and a handful of shells lay on the desk and he was strapping a Webley-Fosbery revolver into a holster across his waistcoat.

"Frank, what the hell is going on?" Kitty was unnerved by the look in Frank's eyes. The door opened behind her and the long, pale face of Alston Holleran appeared around the door frame, closely followed by the russet countenance of Eldon Sledge.

"Mum, Grandad, we're in great danger. Everything has gone wrong." A sheen of perspiration glistened on Frank's upper lip and he seemed to be moving at double quick pace.

"The match? But the second half hasn't even started yet. The squaring isn't even due to happen yet?" Kitty glanced at the clock on the wall then back to her son.

"He isn't playing. Cookson...he's vanished. Says he won't play for City again."

A silence descended as the consequences of the situation sunk in.

"Did you manage to warn the Chinese? Tell them to pull the bets?" Kitty spoke slowly, anticipating and dreading the answer.

"I only found out myself when I got to Elland Road. Ti Xi probably has thousands wagered. Tens of thousands."

Kitty Holleran's usual tough Armley demeanour vanished and her face crumpled into tears.

"It's bad. Very bad, I admit. But I have a plan." Frank raised both hands to stop his grandfather from speaking. "You all need to listen to me." Glancing beyond Mr.Sledge, Holleran spotted the shadow of Arthur Rowley on the frosted glass of the door.

"Arthur, go downstairs and lock up the pub please." He paused, until the shadow shifted without acknowledgement.

"Alright now, listen to me, and we may still get out of this alive."

Kitty Holleran sobbed and Eldon Sledge breathed heavily. Only the eldest member of the Holleran family seemed unaffected and impassive.

"The Chinese will have someone at Elland Road but they don't know who our inside man was. All they knew was that there were to be two penalty kicks and a dismissal in the last thirty minutes." Frank Holleran checked the clock on the wall. "They won't know for another half an hour that those things aren't happening. At that point I'm guessing they'll telephone Ti Xi. If he sends men from Manchester, that's another two hours until they get to Armley. Mum, Grandad, you need to leave immediately. Go to Aunty Clara's in Wales, you'll be safe there."

Holleran raised his hand again to quell the objections from his mother and grandfather.

"Listen to me please!" Holleran reached into the pocket of his overcoat to retrieve an envelope. He took out a single sheet of paper, opened it and tore off the top third.

"Mr. Sledge..."

Eldon Sledge stepped forward and Holleran handed him the torn slip of paper.

"Take this to our man at the GPO. Get him to check the files and provide you with an address for this telephone number. You'll then go there and collect Charlie Cookson. He will be our guest until next week's game against Hull."

"What if he won't come Frank?" Sledge folded the paper and slipped it into his top pocket.

"He will. You'll make him see sense." Holleran picked up a pistol from the desk and handed it to Sledge.

"We'll hold Cookson at the place you have the boy. Next Saturday, we'll deliver him to the Elland Road enclosure, where he'll do what he was meant to do today. At that point we own him, he's complicit, and will have to keep playing our game until we've paid back the Chinese all we owe."

"But what about today? We've lost even more of Ti Xi's money, for God's sake Frank, they took my finger..." Tears streaked down Kitty Holleran's face and her lip trembled as she looked at her son.

"I'll be here when they come. They're not stupid. If they kill me, then they've lost their money. If I can convince them that we can still deliver, I hope we can turn things around." The shaking of his hands betrayed Frank's confidence in the plan.

"What about the boy?" Alston Holleran stood with his arms folded, looking critically at his grandson, who turned away, running his fingers through his hair, rummaging in a filing cabinet, looking for nothing.

"The child is too big a risk. It's unfortunate but as we all know, there is collateral damage in every war," he muttered, almost ashamed to utter the words.

"No!" Alston Holleran smashed both fists on the desk. "The child was taken for a reason. To harvest his blood, to keep us all safe. Killing the child will render the spell useless!"

"No more magic Dad! I've had enough! Did your spells and charms prevent all this?" Kitty Holleran waved her bandaged hand in front of her father's face, causing him to take a step back.

"My charms brought Frank home to us, as they have countless Armley boys over the last four years. They've protected us from this yellow peril since you lost their opium Kitty, and it was your injury that forced Clem to appear again. It was then he told me we needed a stronger charm, that we needed the boy."

"Clem...bloody Clem. Dad! Your stupid magic is going to be what gets us all killed." Kitty threw her hands to her face and turned to leave.

"Mum, take this." Frank held out an Enfield pistol. "Go and pack. You too Grandad. Mr. Sledge and I will do what needs to be done here."

Frank Holleran waved the three of them from his office then slumped down in a chair behind his desk and began loading shells into the Webley-Fosbery automatic revolver with trembling fingers.

He replaced the pistol in the shoulder holster and headed past the pub's upstairs living quarters, from where he could hear the raised voices of his grandfather and mother, arguing about magic and child murder as they threw clothes and belongings into a trunk ahead of their flight to safety.

Frank clumped down the wooden stairs and into the empty bar, from where he heard the crank of the car engine, as Mr.Sledge set off to track down the GPO Clerk who would lead them to Cookson.

Glancing to the right he noticed the pub's side door slightly ajar.

"Arthur! Arthur...Didn't I ask you to lock up the bar? We'll have the kids in here stealing the empty pop bottles again. Arthur?"

Frank walked to the door and looked out onto the cobbled yard.

"Arthur? Are you out there?" But the yard was empty aside from a greasy brown rat which scurried away into the darkness. There would be no shift for Arthur to work tonight, probably best he's made himself scarce, Frank reflected as he closed the door and slid the bolts into place. He walked across to the bar and turned down the gas mantle, reducing the light to a dim glow, still listening to the angry, panicked voices of his family members in the rooms above. Frank removed a bottle of Scotch from behind the bar, unscrewed the top and took a long swig. He pulled up a bar stool, removed his gun, placed it on the bar, and turned to face the door, preparing himself for the storm that he knew was fast approaching over the hills from the west.

Chapter 32

Frank Holleran was halfway down the bottle of Scotch
when they came. He'd left the pub door open and was sat
directly opposite, the pistol resting on the table in front
of him when they entered. A slight man in his early
thirties wearing a grey suit who introduced himself as
Chee Ho, and two Boo-how-doy soldiers.

"Gentlemen, I was expecting you." Holleran made no
attempt to reach for his gun, and Ho seemed unworried
by its presence, though the henchmen instinctively
reached into their overcoats to display the shoulder
holsters containing their long-barrelled German Luger
pistols.

"Do you have a telephone here, Mr Holleran?"Chee
Ho looked around the empty saloon bar. "Mr. Ti Xi is
still engaged in the search for his grandson, but he would
welcome a conversation with you."

Holleran stood unsteadily and took a final swig from
the liquor bottle, then nodded to the door beside the bar.
The three Chinese followed as he limped up the narrow
wooden staircase and into the deserted bookies office at
the top of the stairs.

Frank Holleran nodded to the three phones on the
long desk.

"Take your pick."

Chee Ho picked up the closest telephone set and
removed a piece of paper from his jacket pocket, then
carefully dialled the numbers while glancing back at the
note.

He screwed up his eyes as the call connected, then began speaking in noisy staccato blasts of his undecipherable language.

"Mr. Ti Xi." He held the telephone set out and Frank edged forward and took it from him.

"Hello, Ti Xi..."

The three Chinese looked on as Frank pressed the receiver to his ear, hearing only crackles.

"Hello, are you there Ti Xi? You wanted to speak to me." Frank removed the receiver from his ear and banged it on the desk, then once again pressed it against his head. The Chinese continued to look on impassively.

"Tell me what happened Mr.Holleran." A faint voice crackled down the line.

"What can I say? I'm sorry. Our inside man, the City player, picked up an injury just before the match. I wasn't even aware myself until I arrived at the ground. These things happen in professional sport unfortunately. Beyond our control, I suppose. Rest assured though, that I'll personally ensure the player is fit for the game next Saturday and will deliver the fix as agreed. And in future games too. Believe me Ti Xi, with this player under our control, we can control the outcome of matches right through the season. It won't take long at all to pay back the amount we owe you..."

Chee Ho raised his eyebrows and smirked and Holleran realised the terror he felt was obviously apparent.

"So, again, Ti Xi, please accept my heartfelt apologies for what happened today, and rest assured, I WILL put this right. You can rely on me."

Holleran paused and listened to the crackles on the line. The three Chinese continued to stare at him, and he suspected the connection was lost and his impassioned speech had been wasted.

"Hello, Ti Xi...hello. Are you there?"

"Please put Mr Ho back on the line." The faint voice again crackled from the receiver.

"He wants you." Holleran held out the phone and Chee Ho stepped forward.

"Sit down Mr. Holleran." Ho pointed at a desk chair and one of the Boo-how-doy pulled it back and motioned for him to sit.

Ho pressed the telephone receiver to his ear and again narrowed his eyes. Again, he spoke in loud sudden bursts of his undecipherable tongue, but this time his contribution to the conversation was limited to one word responses.

Frank Holleran felt his heart pounding as he watched Ho, aware of the presence of the Boo-how-doy soldiers behind him.

Eventually, Ho spat out a single word, nodded and replaced the receiver in its cradle.

"Mr Holleran. My employer asked me to establish which is your good foot." He turned to face the seated figure of Frank Holleran.

"My good foot?" Frank smiled. The question was unexpected, but he was now starting to believe that he would be spared after today's disaster.

"I believe you are lame in one of your feet?" Chee Ho and the Boo-how-doy soldiers all looked down at Holleran's calfskin Oxford shoes.

"Yes. I lost three toes from my left foot in the war." Holleran also looked down, slowly waggling his left shoe to emphasise his restricted movement.

The presence of a strong hand on each shoulder caused Frank's body to tense and he looked up slowly to see Chee Ho remove the pliers from his jacket pocket.

An arm tightened around his throat as he twisted in his seat and Ho stepped forward.

"In China, we believe in equilibrium Mr. Holleran, so we'll help you address your physical misbalance. From now on, you're going to have two bad feet."

Chapter 33

Robert Meredith threw a hunk of coal into the hearth and poked the fire into life, casting a glow across the small, stone-walled bar of the Timble Inn.

"Last piece tonight Barnaby. I'll let it burn down after." He raised his voice to rouse the old man in the corner from his slumber.

"You want that filling?" He nodded to a pewter mug on the table. Glancing towards the rain lashed window pane, the old man smiled and raised his tankard.

"I think I could be persuaded Bob, aye, go on then."

"Filthy night out there Bob. They've given out snow for later." A middle-aged man sitting at the bar in mud-splashed galoshes and a deer stalker hat shuddered as the wind rattled the window frame.

"Happen you might be right. Cold enough." Robert Meredith yanked at a pump until the foaming ale cascaded down the sides of the tankard.

"Snow you say, Wilf?" Barnaby's voice was barely audible from the corner.

"Aye, that's what they say Barnaby. I don't know though."

"It's cold enough. Cheers Bob." Barnaby took hold of his drink and looked again at the window, and the silence in the bar was disturbed only by the wind howling down the chimney and the coal crackling in the fireplace.

Ten minutes later, Wilfred Spring stood stiffly, drained his drink and was about to reach for his overcoat, when the heavy wooden pub door opened slowly and a chill wind swirled into the bar, followed by a stranger, shivering violently and soaked from head to toe by the icy rain. The three men in the bar stared, silently, their mouths wide with surprise. Strangers were rare at any time at the Timble inn, let alone on a filthy December Saturday at 9pm.

The young man edged into the bar and removed his cap, his hair saturated beneath. He swallowed hard and was shaking so much that he seemed to be rendered temporarily mute, his eyelids twitching as he grew accustomed to the dim light and noticed the three men observing his entry.

"Are you okay son? Here, let me get you a tot of something to warm you..." Bob Meredith hurried behind the bar and returned to hand the young man a measure of rum. The three Timble men watched as the stranger raised the glass to his lips with shaking hands.

"Where have you come from? I didn't hear a motor car."

The young man shook his head and grimaced as he threw back the liquor.

"Otley." He stammered and looked down at the pool of rain water that was forming around him.

"You walked from Otley in this weather?" It's six miles." Bob Meredith and Wilf Spring exchanged dubious glances.

"Used to walk it in all weather when I was a boy. Once walked from Otley in four foot of snow..." Barnaby called from his seat in the corner as he put on a pair of spectacles to better observe the young man.

"I'm here to see Charlie." Bob Meredith froze as the young man uttered the words and turned slowly towards him.

"Charlie?

"Charlie Cookson... He told me his uncle owned this pub ...it's a special place for him and Percy.... I served with Percy in the Pals, he's my friend..." He stammered and spluttered the words and shook visibly. His face was purple with cold.

"Charlie Cookson, the Leeds City player?" Wilf Spring was smiling, shaking his head.

"Yes, Charlie. I work at Elland Road. He told me."

Wilf was laughing now and turning to Bob Meredith behind the bar.

"Have we got any footballers in tonight Bob? I haven't noticed any, have you?"

Bob looked the young man up and down with a mixture of suspicion and pity.

"I think someone has been having you on lad, pulling your leg, as they say."

"No, Charlie told me. Timble Inn. He said I could come here, when Percy gets home..." But the two men were shaking their heads and the old man in the corner was asking who Charlie Cookson was, and Arthur knew now that he wouldn't find Charlie here.

"I'm sorry. I must have made a mistake." The young man turned, replaced his sodden cap on his head and opened the door, and the wind howled and blew freezing sleet into the bar.

"Where are you going now? Not back to Otley?"

The young man turned up the collar of his overcoat.

"The last omnibus to Leeds is at 10.30. I'll catch it if I run. I'm sorry to have bothered you."

The door closed behind him, and Bob and Wilf looked at each other in silence.

Freezing water splashed up Arthur's legs with every laboured step as he jogged along the rutted track which served as the main street of the hamlet of Timble. He was so cold, he was unsure that he could even stimulate his stiff legs into motion, and tried to dispel the thought of a night sleeping rough in the freezing Wharfedale countryside.

He paused as he approached the junction with the Blubberhouses road and reached into his coat for his pocket watch, but was unable to see its face in the darkness. He removed his cap and squeezed out the water, then replaced it on his head, took a deep breath and set off running.

He'd taken only ten steps when he caught a sound in the wind which caused him to slow his pace. A human voice or maybe a farmyard beast, a cow or sheep complaining at the weather?

He paused and listened. This time there was no doubt. Arthur. Shouted from somewhere in the darkness behind him.

"Hello?" Arthur stopped and looked down the lane towards Timble, to see a figure in a rain cape approaching, jogging through the slush-filled puddles towards him. An athletic gait and smiling face. Charlie Cookson.

"Arthur...my God, look at the state of you. I'm sorry. I saw you from the upstairs window. My uncle is under strict instructions to make sure no one knows I'm here."

"They know. Or they will soon." Arthur shifted his weight from foot to foot as the rain poured down his face.

"Who? Mr.O'Connell?"

"No. Frank Holleran. He has your phone number and someone at the GPO who can link it to an address. They'll be here soon. I heard them. They're going to make you play in the Hull game next week."

Charlie Cookson pulled the hood of the cape back to reveal his face.

"They're trying to get me to fix games, Arthur. I can't do that. If I get caught I'll go to jail, and Percy will have no one. I need money quickly to get him out of hospital and pay for his care. I've been offered £75 to sign on for Coventry, and £6 a week wage, but Mr.O'Connell won't let me leave. If I stay at City, I'll end up in jail, or dead."

Arthur looked at the pitted gravel of the Blubberhouses road, the rainwater trickling down his face like a cascade of tears.

"Before she died, our mum used to say that one good deed outweighs ten bad ones. Do you think that's true?" Arthur looked up at Charlie Cookson.

"If she said it Arthur, I'm sure it must be right."

Arthur reached into his overcoat and produced a thick manila envelope, darkened by moisture.

"Take this. I think it will help you."

"What is it Arthur?"

"Mr. Cribbins gave it to my brother for safekeeping. I'm sure he'd want you to have it. I have to go now." Arthur began backing away into the darkness.

"Arthur, my uncle has a motor car. He'll get me away and he can give you a ride too."

But Arthur was already running, turning to shout 'Look after Percy', as he splashed through the puddles, heading downhill towards Otley, facing into the storm.

Chapter 34

Arthur rinsed the horsehair brush under the tap and watched as the thick red liquid splashed into the sink. Taking the brush in his left hand he picked up an ashtray in his right and brushed the contents into a dustbin.

"Mrs. Holleran, I think the bin needs emptying," he shouted, but the bar was empty. His nostrils twitched at a foul smell emanating from the bin, a smell he knew but couldn't place, and he pushed his hand into the mix of ash and cigarette butts and bottle tops and matches and withdrew it, holding it in front of his eyes, sniffing at the gloopy, brown-red mess on his fingers.

He heard the pub door open.

"We're closed." He shouted, and was pleased that he didn't stammer, his voice was clear and true. He almost sounded confident.

He heard a chair scrape. The customer hadn't heeded his warning, so he walked into the tap room to tell them that hours were still restricted, with beer still in short supply, plus the new restrictions imposed due to the influenza epidemic.

At first he struggled to place the boy. Blond hair shaved at the sides but left in an unruly mop with a thick fringe which stuck to the perspiration on his forehead. He grinned, white teeth prominent below thin lips and sunken cheeks pitted with acne scars.

"Hello Arthur."

"I remember you. I thought you'd gone away."

"Not yet. He needs us." The boy beckoned Arthur to the side door of the pub and he followed, careful not to step in the trail of blood which was dripping from the boy's stomach.

Out of the door, through the cobbled yard, down the ginnel to the mill pond, round the right hand side of the water. The boy leading the way, looking back at Arthur, smiling with his prominent white teeth, his pock marked face, his bullet shredded stomach.

They reached the outhouses of the woollen mill on Carr Crofts, the old warehouses and stables.

"Down there." The boy pointed the way, between stone buildings with boarded windows and padlocked wooden doors.

"He'll show you."

"Who?" Arthur turned but the boy was gone.

Down the cobbled alley, past the stacked fleeces, the sunken pits of tanning fluid, the stench making his eyes stream with acid tears.

"Who?"

But then he knew. An archway in a single storey building, heavy wooden doors with peeling yellow paint. A large black dog sat in the centre of the double doors.

The large black dog stood as Arthur approached and turned and squeezed itself through a narrow gap in the doors. He followed, blinking in the gloom, the dog now invisible in the darkness.

A child's voice. "Here. Quickly. I'm dying."

Arthur turned and threw open the doors. The barn was bathed in light and the boy, tied to a chair, smiled.

"I knew you'd come Arthur."

Arthur Rowley sat upright in his bed. His face was burning and his body was soaked in sweat or rain or both and he was still wearing his boots, the wet leather seeping into the mattress. He shivered, though his body felt like it was on fire. Still dark in the December dawn, he climbed slowly from his bed, steadying himself on the dressing table as the room reeled and span. Through the bedroom door, clinging to the banister, he stumbled down the stairs. The blurred figure of his brother, clasping a mug of tea in front of the hearth.

"Arthur! Arthur! I need to speak to you..."

Arthur didn't pause. Through the door, onto the cobbles of Willoughby Grove, running now, his feet sliding on the wet pavement, his jacketless, sweat soaked body suddenly cold in the chill morning air, his brother's voice echoing along the terraced street, turning left into Domestic Street, heading downhill to the viaduct, the tram terminus and the road past the big house, His Majesty's Prison, the road to Armley.

Chapter 35

Frank Holleran lifted his head from the bar table, the persistent knocking rousing him from his fitful sleep. He moved his right arm and an empty Scotch bottle tumbled onto the stone flagged floor of the White Horse. The knocking on the front door of the pub continued and Holleran glanced at a brass clock on the wall, salvaged from a fire at Antwerp mills. Twenty to ten. Sunday morning.

Frank's head throbbed and he struggled to swallow, but those symptoms were relegated to minor inconveniences when he tried to stand, placing his right foot on the floor caused him to scream out in pain and he slumped to his knees and crawled across the cold stone floor of the pub.

Hauling himself upright, he slid the large bolt on the pub door, leaving the chain in place. Through the crack in the door, he saw the anxious red face of Eldon Sledge peering back at him.

"Frank?"

Holleran closed the door to remove the chain, then swayed, holding the door frame to support himself as the door swang open.

"Frank, what happened?" Mr.Sledge took a step back and regarded his boss with wide eyes.

"The Chinese took my toe nails. My good foot too. Where is he? Have you taken him to the place?"

"My God, Frank." Sledge looked down at his boss's bare feet, the left one missing three toes, the right one a bloody mass, and grimaced.

"Cookson? Have you taken him straight to the place?"

Sledge edged into the pub without speaking.

"I managed to convince Ti Xi that we can still deliver the fix next Saturday, that's why they only took my toe nails, this time anyway..."

"Frank..." Eldon Sledge avoided eye contact and shuffled nervously, touching the brim of his cap, tics that Holleran recognised from numerous police interrogations.

"Tell me, Mr.Sledge."

"He's gone Frank." Eldon Sledge now met Holleran's panicked stare. "I only got the address this morning. A pub out past Otley. I was there first thing. The landlord denied knowing Cookson, wouldn't say a thing, even when I busted his nose and snapped both his arms. As I was leaving, I saw this old fellow working a field, kept looking over. Anyway, after I slipped him a couple of quid, he told me Cookson was there, but he left last night after some young bloke turned up looking for him."

Holleran's face was drained of colour and Sledge helped him back to his bar stool.

"Described the lad as dark haired, early twenties, shaking hands and what he called dead man's eyes."

"Fucking Arthur." Holleran banged his clenched fists on the table. "How did he know? That's it, we're finished. We can't risk trying to involve any other City players at this stage. You're looking at a dead man, Mr.Sledge."

Holleran motioned to Sledge to retrieve a new bottle of Scotch from behind the bar, but the big man hesitated.

"How about a cup of tea boss? I could do with one. And I'll fetch a bowl of water, have a look at that foot."

By the time the kettle had begun to emit its shrill whistle, Eldon Sledge could hear Holleran calling from the bar. He poured the boiling water into a steel bowl, into which he also poured half a bottle of disinfectant.

"Boss?" Sledge could see a dramatic shift in Holleran's demeanour. When he'd left the bar, he'd seemed defeated. Now he turned in his seat, with what could even be described as a half-smile on his face.

"I've got a plan, Mr.Sledge. It's risky but might get us out of this whole mess."

"I'll go fetch the tea Frank."

Sledge shambled back into the bar clutching two steaming mugs, and Holleran winced as he dipped his foot into the bowl of water.

"What's the plan boss?" Sledge knelt and gently lifted Holleran's foot from the bowl, using a cloth to carefully dap at the congealed blood around his toes.

"I saw the boy as a liability, but now I'm thinking he could actually be an asset. My Grandad's Wiseman lunacy might have actually saved us...ah Jesus Christ!" Frank clenched his teeth and grimaced as Eldon Sledge dabbed at an exposed nail root with the cloth."

"Sorry boss, I need to clean it up though or it'll get infected. You don't want to lose any more toes...go on, tell me the plan." Sledge knelt over the bowl of red water and looked up at Holleran.

"Ti Xi cares more about the boy than the money we owe. What if we were to find the boy, send him home? What if we received a tip off that the Folans kidnapped the boy in revenge for Ti Xi taking back the opium and killing some of their lads? Maybe they planned to trade the boy for the opium?! Yes, that's it...we found him in one of their warehouses and rescued him! It will certainly buy us some more time to get another City player on the books. He might even write off the debt!" Holleran took a swig of his tea.

"Fetch me the Scotch, Mr.Sledge, then help me up to the office so I can call Ti Xi. Then go to the boy, he's blindfolded isn't he?"

"Bound, gagged and blindfolded boss. He'll be groggy too. And hungry, he's not been fed since yesterday. He's not seen me though, don't worry."

"That's good. Take your chemicals, enough to knock him out for a couple of hours. Bring him into the pub, put him in my mother's bed. Then take his school cap, satchel and the ropes he's bound with, and go to Bradford. Go to the Folan's warehouse at Apperley Bridge and hide them there. Not too well, but not too obvious either. I'm guessing Ti Xi will send some of his boys to check our story, so we need to make sure they find them. Not only could this get us off the hook with the yellow men, but it could also wipe out the fucking Folans!" Holleran smiled as Mr.Sledge handed him the liquor bottle.

"Help me up those stairs Mr.Sledge. I need to break the good news to our little Chinese friend!"

Chapter 36

"You have the boy there Mr.Holleran? He is safe and well?" The quiet voice on the phone for once displayed a hint of emotion.

"He's been drugged, sedated, Ti Xi. He's hungry and thirsty too, but other than that, seems unharmed. Don't worry. He's here with me. Sleeping in my mother's bed as we speak."

"He was in Bradford you say?"

"I put the word out as I promised you." Frank Holleran took a swig of Scotch, savouring the moment, Ti Xi for once hanging on his every word. "One of my contacts gave us information which led us to a warehouse next to the canal. My understanding is that it's owned by a family called the Folans..." Frank paused, allowing the name to register.

"Folan? From Bradford?"

"That's right Ti Xi. There were three brothers. One died in France. The other two are trying to expand their..."

"They are the men who tried to sell me my own opium Mr. Holleran."

"Oh...well..that's interesting..." Frank Holleran took another swig of Scotch while he waited for Ti Xi to draw his own conclusions.

"Mr. Holleran, thank you. I will set off now and should be in Leeds in a couple of hours to collect the boy. You will also provide the address where he was found. I can assure you that my retribution will be swift and brutal.

Believe me, you will hear no more of these Folans." Ti Xi's anger was tangible even down the crackling telephone line.

"I don't blame you Ti Xi. Involving a child in a business dispute is a despicable act. Those involved need to pay a very high price." Frank Holleran smiled to himself. Two problems solved at a stroke.

"And Mr.Holleran..." Ti Xi spoke slowly and quietly. "My apologies for the events of last night. My mental state was not good. I should have been more patient, and am sure you will make amends for our lost wager next Saturday. I will see you in Leeds soon."

The line clicked before Holleran could respond. He took a swig from the whisky bottle and pulled up a chair, extending his legs and looking down at his mangled feet as the pub door opened with a bang and he heard the uncharacteristically rapid beat of Mr. Sledge's footsteps on the stairs, preceding his appearance, red faced and breathing heavily, in the doorway.

"Where's the boy?" Frank Holleran felt the nausea rising, and his heartbeat race as Eldon Sledge began to shake his head.

"He's gone Frank."

"Gone? Where? How?" Frank stood, now forgetting the pain in his feet.

"We had him in one of the old carding sheds at the woollen mill. Tied up, as I told you. He couldn't have escaped...someone must have found him Frank. He's gone."

Mr.Sledge had worked for the Holleran's for thirty years. He'd watched Frank grow up, and he now took a step back, expecting an explosion of rage and violence. Instead, Frank Holleran stood and steadied himself, his hand on the desk, and shuffled round to open a drawer.

"Mr.Sledge, thanks for everything you've done for me and my family. I wish you well for the future."

"What...Frank...you're sacking me? I'm sorry but it's not my fault the boy has gone..."

"I'm not sacking you Mr.Sledge. It's over."

Frank Holleran removed the Webley-Fosbery automatic pistol from the drawer, placed it carefully on the desk in front of him and sat down.

"We're finished Mr.Sledge...I'm finished."

Chapter 37

"Things are looking up Edgar, look at this!" Eliza Rowley burst through the front door clutching a small bundle wrapped in muslin cloth. "Martha's brother got a pound of cheese and she's sold me a corner...What's the matter?" Eliza's effervescent mood dissipated rapidly as she caught sight of her husband's worried face. Edgar lowered the Sunday Times, raised himself from his armchair and pulled back the net curtains to look out onto the street, without speaking.

"Don't worry about Arthur, love. He'll be back." Eliza rested a hand on his shoulder and Edgar turned round.

"What's he involved himself in Eliza? Magic spells, animal sacrifice, staying out half the night and sleeping in his clothes, then disappearing without a word this morning. His mind seems to have gone completely..."

"I'll just put this cheese on the cold stone in the pantry love. You can have a bit with some lettuce for tea if you'd like?" Eliza set off towards the scullery but was halted by a soft tap on the front door. She and Edgar exchanged worried glances and without thinking she muttered "That's not a policeman's knock," then immediately regretted it as she caught her husband's eye.

Eliza opened the door and took a step back in surprise.

"Who is it 'Liza?" Edgar approached and peered over her shoulder, to see a small figure on the doorstep wearing a schoolcap and blazer.

"Are you Mr.Rowley?" the boy was ten or eleven, of oriental appearance with a pale, grimy, tear stained face and dark rings beneath his eyes.

"I am yes, and who are you?" Edgar and his wife stared down at the child, whose lip trembled as his eyes shifted nervously, scanning both sides of the street. "It's okay, you're safe here. Who are you and where are your parents?"

The boy looked at the floor and a heavy tear fell onto the flagstones.

"Come in, out of the cold. Let's get you warmed up..." Eliza opened the door and the boy nervously climbed the two steps and entered the small living room, his eyes still flitting left and right.

"He told me to come here." The boy stood in the centre of the room and fumbled in the pocket of his blazer to retrieve a sheet of lined paper which he handed to Edgar.

Edgar Rowley read his own name and address and handed it to his wife, his own lip now trembling.

"Arthur's hand writing."

Edgar turned away to prevent the child from seeing his distress and Eliza pulled out a chair from the dining table.

"You sit down here and let's get you a cup of tea. What did you say your name was?"

"I'm Li Yuan. My friends call me Li." The child whispered as he sat down, staring at the floor.

"Alright Li, you make yourself at home while I put the kettle on. You can tell Mr.Rowley all about it." Eliza squeezed her husband's arm and he bit his lip and dabbed his eyes, then pulled up a chair to sit opposite the boy.

"The man who gave you this, he's my brother, Arthur. How do you know him?" Edgar smiled and leant across the table to rub the boys hand.

"I don't know him sir. He came for me this morning. He freed me."

"Freed you?" Edgar felt his skin prickle at the boy's words.

"I was in a place, it was dark and cold and there were rats and mice, I could hear them moving. I was tied to a chair and I couldn't see. I had some cloth in my mouth. I couldn't talk..."

Edgar tried to suppress the feeling of horror he knew his face was betraying.

"Who put you there Li? Who took you to that place?"

The boy shook his head and now his tears came in a flood and Edgar stood and put his arm around him as Eliza looked on from the scullery doorway, her eyes wide with shock.

"Who put you there Li?" Edgar whispered gently and rubbed the child's back.

"I don't know sir. I remember leaving school then nothing until I was in the back of a motor car, but my hands were tied and I had a sack over my head. I couldn't see. Then I was put in the place." Li Yuan blinked and shook visibly as he recounted his ordeal.

"When you were in the place, the people who took you, did they...come to you?" Edgar almost dreaded the response.

"Yes sir, they came twice a day and fed me soup with a spoon. Then they put a pin in me."

"A pin?" They put a pin in you?"

"In my arm. It pricked me. It hurt." Li Yuan slowly removed his blazer and unbuttoned his shirt cuff, then rolled up his sleeve to reveal a bruised forearm, dappled with bloodied indentations.

"My God..." Eliza turned back to the kitchen, dabbing at her eyes.

"The man who rescued you, my brother Arthur, where is he now?" Edgar felt his own eyes sting with tears as he looked at the trembling child.

"He's gone."

"Gone? Where has he gone Li?"

The boy stood and pointed out of the window, in the direction of Domestic Street.

"He took me from the place, then we walked for half an hour. He had to give me a piggy-back ride as I was too tired. We went to a park over there, there was a bandstand, but the band wasn't playing..."

The boy turned back from the window.

"That's Holbeck Moor, the park you went to. Is he still there, my brother?"

Li Yuan shook his head.

"We sat on a bench near the bandstand sir. The man, your brother, didn't say anything. I didn't understand why we were there. I was cold. Then he asked me if I could hear the birds singing."

Edgar blinked back tears. "Then what happened Li?"

"I listened and I could hear them singing. I told him I could, and he nodded and smiled. He smiled but he looked sad. Then he gave me your address and told me to come here. He shook my hand and said good luck."

"And then Li?" Eliza stood above Edgar who was looking at the floor in silence.

"He told me he still couldn't hear them, the birds. Then he said goodbye and he walked away."

"What do you think that means Edgar?" Eliza leant forward, her hand on her husband's shoulder and spoke softly in his ear.

Edgar remained silent, then reached up and gripped Eliza's hand.

"I think it means...I have an awful feeling that we'll never see my brother again love."

.

Part 3 -September 1919

Chapter 38

"Mark my words Jack, the Union Triple Alliance's next move will be a general strike, closely followed by a Bolshevik style revolution, followed by total anarchy." Joseph O'Connell clung to his hat with his right hand and tried to maintain the light of his cigar with his left, as the Charabanc bumped along the Ashby road, north of Tamworth.

"You don't really believe that Joe?" Jack Whiteman ducked his head behind the shoulders of fellow director Samuel Glover seated on the bench in front, and shouted to prevent his words being lost in the late summer breeze as the vehicle headed north after Leeds City's 4-2 victory at Wolverhampton.

"Believe it? Of course I do. The Russians didn't see revolution coming until it was too late and look at them now. The Czar murdered and the rest of the Romanovs imprisoned God knows where." O'Connell sucked on his cigar and spat into the wind.

"Bloody NUR aren't going to back down, when even the police force and the army joins them on strike. Believe me, there'll be no more trains until Lloyd George bows to their greed. We'll be stuck on these bloody buses in the depths of winter. We'll freeze to death travelling to an away fixture!"

"If we're still in the league in Winter." Jack Whiteman coughed and awaited the predictable response from the Leeds City chairman.

"Don't worry on that score Jack. Alderman Clarke and the mayor are meeting with that bloody busybody Clegg at the FA this weekend. They'll explain why we're unable to turn over the documents they've asked for, and also try and find out exactly what it is they've got hold of."

"What about us though Joe? Even if the club survives, they're going to push for all the board to go." Whiteman was concerned at the negative impact any public scandal would have on his other business interests.

"Unfortunately Jack, if the directors have to become the collateral damage which saves City, then so be it. I doubt it will come to that though, and in terms of penalising the club, what are they going to do? Kick us out of the league? It would be unthinkable for one of England's greatest cities to be without a football team would it not? It will never happen, believe me." O'Connell took a final draw on his cigar then removed it from his mouth and flicked it from the charabanc.

"What's the bloody hold up now? Oh for God's sake, not another stop to pick up roadside tramps..." O'Connell folded his arms and pushed his chin deep into his muffler as the charabanc drew to a halt at a crossroads outside the village of Measham.

"They're not tramps Joe. They're mostly working men trying to get back north. I must admit though, it's getting a bit crowded now. Six to a bench at the front..." O'Connell stood up and watched as the driver negotiated with a clutch of men stood at the roadside.

The charabanc door opened with a clunk and half a dozen men began to clamber aboard, the City players at the front standing and jostling for position with their colleagues further along the bus.

"I hope we're charging these buggers." O'Connell grumbled, raising his head and observing the newcomers. Suddenly Whiteman felt O'Connell stiffen, before hauling himself to a standing position, an electricity of fury coursing through his body.

"What's the matter Joe?" Whiteman stood too, his gaze following the extended arm of the chairman, pointing down the charabanc at a figure skulking at the rear of the newcomers, a flat cap pulled low over his eyes.

"Not him! Not that man! Not on my bus! Get him off, now!"

The players began to turn on their benches, looking back at O'Connell, smiling, shaking their heads at their chairman's fury.

"Who is that chap Joe? I can't see his face." Jack Whiteman craned his neck as the players now began to stand too, trying to catch a glimpse of the man, who ducked his head and tried to crouch on the step, next to the driver.

"Get him off. Off my bus now. If I could get down there to the front, I'd fucking kill him."

The whole charabanc was now turning, looking from the chairman to the stranger, who pulled his cap lower and stumbled from the bus.

"Fuck you! Bastard traitor! I'll have you killed you bastard..." O'Connell shook his fist and spat as the charabanc engine growled into life and slowly pulled away from the man, now standing alone on the roadside.

"Joe...that wasn't..?" Whiteman looked back at the stranger who had now removed his cap to watch the bus depart.

"Charlie fucking Cookson. The man who somehow got hold of Cribbins' books to force through a move to Coventry. The man whose actions could yet sound the death knell for our great club."

Chapter 39

"As final working days go," Clifford Ellington leant back in his seat at the Yorkshire Evening Post offices in Albion Street. "I'd describe yours as quite memorable."

Edgar Rowley smiled as he entered the office clutching a brown leather briefcase.

"How did it go at the Metropole?" Clifford liberated a bottle of whiskey and two glasses from his desk drawer and began to pour.

"I can't believe it's happened. That they've kicked City out of the league. Closed the club down." Edgar pulled up a chair and sat opposite Clifford. "The players were all there. I felt sorry for them."

"Why feel sorry? They'll be earning a damned sight more than you will as a teacher...and me as a hack who can't afford to retire!" Clifford swigged off his drink and poured another.

"It just felt like a slave market. They all stood there in the Metropole's banqueting room and watched as they were sold off to the highest bidder. Billy Mcleod fetched the best price, £1250 to Notts County. Millership, Bainbridge and Hampson all went for a thousand. Poor Franny Chipperfield only fetched a hundred quid from the Wednesday."

"Hmmm, slaves earning £4 a week eh?" Both men smiled and raised their glasses.

"I have something for you...a thank you, for helping me back in '14 when I knew nothing about journalism or working on a newspaper." Edgar reached into his briefcase and retrieved a rectangle wrapped in brown paper.

Clifford laughed. "I doubt you'd have ever left that school if you'd known you'd end up trailing round the market reporting on which stalls had lamb or butter for sale. Watching City win the league then implode. And helping a gout-ridden old crime reporter..."

"Open it." Edgar passed the parcel across the desk and Clifford swilled his glass before taking hold of the parcel, tentatively tearing open the string and brown paper.

A dark wood frame was revealed, surrounding an Evening Post front page, covered by a thin layer of glass. Clifford held it at arm's length and read the familiar headline.

'Witchcraft Link to Grenade Attack Pub.'

Clifford smiled and shook his head.

"Forty five years a journalist, and my only award came from a story fed to me by a school teacher pretending to be a reporter."

"It was your story Cliff. You did the work. You deserved the award. You need to celebrate it, remember it. Get it up on the office wall." Edgar walked to the window and looked out onto the early afternoon bustle of Albion Street.

"Edgar..."

Edgar Rowley turned to see Clifford pull a blue Leeds City Police file from his drawer and his heart sank. He knew this routine, had been through it half a dozen times over the last nine months.

"I'm sorry old chap, on your final day, but you've always insisted..."

"Of course. Show me Cliff, I need to know."

Clifford Ellington opened the file and removed a square photograph, glanced at it, then turned it on its head and placed it on the desk in front of Edgar.

Edgar's eyes remained locked on Clifford's for too long, until he forced himself to glance down at the face staring back at him from a mortuary slab.

"Where?"

"They pulled him from the Ouse at Acaster Malbis."

Edgar stared at the boy. Dark hair, a ghostly white face. Thick fringe pushed back from a forehead scored with a bloody gash. Thin lips curled back to reveal a gap-toothed rictus grin. First signs of a nascent moustache. Late teens, early twenties. Someone's son. Someone's brother. But not his.

"It's not Arthur."

Clifford nodded and sighed. "Good. Don't worry Edgar, we'll find him one day. We'll bring him home, lad."

Edgar nodded and turned back to look down upon Albion Street.

"Arthur will come home when he's ready Cliff. When he can hear the birds singing again, that's when he'll come home. Then he'll know that his war is finally over. The day he hears the birdsong on Holbeck Moor again."

More Crime Fiction from Billy Morris –

Bournemouth 90

It's April 1990 and the world is changing. Margaret Thatcher clings to power in the face of poll tax protests, prison riots and sectarian violence in Northern Ireland. The Berlin wall has fallen, South Africa's Apartheid government is crumbling and in the Middle East Saddam Hussein is flexing his muscles, while Iran is still trying to behead Salman Rushdie. In Leeds, United are closing in on a long-awaited return to the first division. Neil Yardsley is heading home after three years away and hoping to go straight. That's the plan, but Neil finds himself being drawn back into a world of football violence, and finds a brother up to his neck in the drug culture of the rave scene. Dark family secrets bubble to the surface as Neil tries to help his brother dodge a gangland death sentence, while struggling to keep his own head above water in a city that no longer feels like home. The pressure is building with all roads leading to the south coast, and a final reckoning on a red-hot Bank Holiday weekend in Bournemouth that no one will ever forget.

Amazon Reviews of Bournemouth 90-

"Fast paced unflinching read."

"Well researched, 'in the know' story."

"Earthy, Leeds-based, Guy Ritchie style underworld thriller."

"The timeline & atmosphere around the build-up and description of that weekend captures just what it was like to be there."

LS92

Two years have passed, but the events of Bournemouth 90 continue to cast a dark shadow over the lives of everyone who travelled south on that hot Bank Holiday weekend. Max Jackson is out of jail and trying to re-establish himself in a Leeds underworld being torn apart by gangland warfare. The Yardsley brothers are still paying the price for their actions, with the spectre of Alan Connolly continuing to haunt them. At Millgarth, Sergeant Andy Barton finds himself in the limelight after Bournemouth, but terrace culture is changing, and police intelligence is struggling to adapt to the new normal of the nineties. At Elland Road, a resurgent United are heading towards their first league title in eighteen years, but a disturbing, malevolent force is threatening to gatecrash the champions' victory party. Old scores are settled and new ones imagined, as the climax to the title showdown becomes a deadly quest for vengeance, forgiveness and redemption. LS92. Dark crime fiction from a time when it was still grim up north.

Amazon Reviews of LS92-

" Fast moving crime thriller which picks up the pace two years on from Bournemouth 90, and captures the changing skyline of 1992 inner city Leeds, with its unforgiving streets, dubious bars and the unique characters of its time."

"If you like crime thrillers with a touch of terrace culture you will enjoy the journey this book takes you on."

"What can you say about a book that you read cover to cover in one session? There's almost no higher praise than that."

Printed in Great Britain
by Amazon

87296001R00099